PAT ROSIER is a former editor of *Broadsheet*, New Zealand's foremost feminist magazine, a former school teacher, and currently earns her living as an organisational consultant. She shares a house at the beach with her partner, Prue Hyman, in Paekakariki on the North Island's Kapiti Coast. Her previous publications include contributions to two poetry collections and, with Myra Hauschild, *Get Used To It! Children of lesbian and gay parents*, also available from Spinifex.

PAT ROSIER

POPPY'S PROGRESS

Spinifex Press Pty Ltd
504 Queensberry Street
North Melbourne, Vic. 3051
Australia

women@spinifexpresss.com.au
http://www.spinifexpress.com.au

First published 2002
Copyright © Pat Rosier

Cover design by Deb Snibson
Typeset by Claire Warren
Printed and bound by McPhersons Printing Group

National Library of Australia
Cataloguing-in-Publication data:

Rosier, Pat, 1942– .
    Poppy's progress.

    ISBN 1 876756 28 4.

    1. Lesbianism – Fiction. 2. Life change events – Fiction.
    3. Interpersonal relationships – Fiction. I. Title.

NZ823.3

Acknowledgements

Special thanks to my partner Prue Hyman for love and support, for reading several drafts and for thinking of the title.

Thank you to Susie Probert who helped with the original idea and read and commented on two drafts.

Thank you to those who read and commented on various versions – Jill Hannah, Jill Livestre, Robyn Sievewright, Jan Thorburn, and Carole Beu – and to all those friends who would like to have read it but were never given the chance.

In Chapter 3 there is a reference to *Maus* by Art Spiegelman (1980, Pantheon Books). According to its cover blurb, *Maus* 'ties together two powerful stories: Vladek's harrowing tale of survival against all odds, delineating the paradox of daily life in the death camps, and the author's account of his tortured relationship with his father'.

1

1999

Poppy looked down at the papers on her desk, hoping to conceal a yawn. She struggled to pay attention to what Mr – uh – Michael's father – was saying. When he paused she looked up, wanting to believe that her attempt at a smile disguised the remnants of that persistent yawn.

'What I can say, Mr – uh – ?'

'Jones.'

'Oh, of course, how silly of me. What I want to tell you, Mr Jones, is that it is a real pleasure to have Michael in my class.'

Poppy was immediately appalled at what she had said. She wasn't looking as desperate as she felt, was she, after three hours of interviews with the parents of the children she had been teaching all year? She couldn't believe she had used the 'real pleasure' cliché, that desperate refuge of teachers groping for something to tell an anxious parent.

'I am glad you like him,' said Mrs Jones. Poppy felt even worse. She had forgotten Michael's mother was there, sitting off to one side nodding while Mr Jones talked.

The school bell rang briefly, signalling the end of the Jones's allotted time with their son's Year Four teacher and the end of the 'meet the teacher' evening. Poppy did her best to move her stiff and tired face muscles into a natural smile, as she stood, thanking the Joneses for coming, shaking his hand and putting out hers to do the same with Mrs Jones, who said, 'Thank you so much.' Poppy had no idea what she was being thanked for. Mr Jones strode out of the room, Mrs Jones turned at the door with a smile and a wave.

'Why, oh why, do I do it? Why do I forget to look at mothers and not talk to them when there's a father there?' Poppy flopped into her chair, shaking her head at herself, and saw Mrs Mudgely in a corner of her mind, wearing her usual quizzical look. 'I know, I know,' she said, 'you should be Ms Mudgely, but I just can't think of you as anything but Mrs M. You just are.'

'Talking to yourself again? Or is there an invisible parent here? Coming for a drink?' Amelia's head in the doorway was joined by Tony's, his up, hers down. 'C'mon Pop, drinks at the Empire.'

'Thanks, but no thanks, I'm practically too tired to drive home over the bridge already. And Mrs Mudgely hasn't had any dinner.' She shook her head to dislodge the vigorously nodding Mrs M. 'Really, I've had quite enough of today and just want to go home and blob. No, Tony, I really don't want to,' as he moved into the room laughing, persuading, nudging her arm.

'Come on, Tony.' Amelia looked offended, or hurt, or something Poppy couldn't figure out, didn't want to figure out. She gathered her bag and coat and walked around Tony and out the door, saying as she went, 'Goodnight, don't drink too much, see you both tomorrow.'

Driving over Auckland's Harbour Bridge in blessedly light traffic, with the North Shore behind her, Poppy let out a big sigh. She hated parent interview evenings, they seemed so disconnected from her days in the classroom and she felt wooden and stilted talking about children she knew well to parents she hardly knew at all. The parents' anxieties were mostly far removed from the immersion in life and learning that she loved so much and experienced every day working with their children.

As she drove down the city side of the bridge, the postcard sight of the city lights and the forest of masts in the marina, all reflected in the still, dark night water, worked their magic, and the tensions of the long day began to fall away. Turning off the motorway towards her favourite place, her house on the lower slopes of Auckland's Maungawhau, Poppy felt almost content. Just her and Mrs Mudgely for the rest of evening, she thought, just what she needed.

By the time she pulled up in her usual street park at the gap in the three-metre-high stone wall rising from the footpath that was her front entrance, she was looking forward to the rest of the evening. The phoenix palm in the corner of her garden stood guard over the neighbourhood as usual and there was a half moon sliding across the sky behind it.

'Bear up, Mrs M, dinner is on the way.' Poppy gathered her bag, coat and umbrella from the back seat, checking carefully that all the car doors were locked. Hearing the phone ringing inside the house, she ran up the steps, turning when it stopped to go back and clear the letterbox of several items of junk mail and a package from her father in England.

The front door unlocked easily for once and she looked around for Mrs Mudgely. 'Please don't sulk tonight,' she muttered, dropping everything on a hall chair, and heading for the kitchen. While she was transferring a plastic pot of left-over soup from the freezer to the microwave, she became aware of a familiar soft rubbing at her ankles.

'Hello Mrs M, I was wondering where you'd got to.' She picked up the cat and rubbed her face in its fur. 'Dinner and the telly for us tonight, and no comments from you about anti-social school teachers who can't be bothered going out for a drink with their colleagues. Just think how late your dinner would have been.'

Later, lying on the sofa with Mrs Mudgely curled purring on her stomach, almost watching a television programme she wasn't interested in, Poppy remembered the package from her father.

'Sorry,' she said to the cat as she moved, 'I'd better find out what the father has sent me.'

Poppy had been eighteen when her parents separated nearly thirty years ago. At the time she had felt like she was being torn in two. They had been a unit, one entity, to her, Mum-and-Dad; for several years she could barely believe they were divorced. That was when she had started to think of them as her mother and her father and calling them Katrina and George.

Katrina had had three partners since that time, though she got married only once more. George had married Susanna in what Poppy thought was far too short a time after the divorce and they had gone to live near her family in North Yorkshire. He had found a job at the Cleveland Natural History Museum in Middlesbrough and been there ever since, conscientiously keeping in touch with Poppy and her brother by letter and phone and with occasional visits. She had always preferred the times she went to England to his visits to New Zealand; it didn't matter so much that his wife wasn't her mother when they were in Yorkshire. The packages still came every three or four months and were usually something not very important, though she knew George put a lot of thought into their contents; it was one of his ways of 'keeping us in each others' lives' as he would say, and Poppy wished she tried harder to find things to send him.

Today's package included two photographs of George and some work colleagues at the museum, two articles from the *Cleveland Times* about local schools – that idea about having children make painting palettes out of newspaper and mixing their own colours was interesting – and a picture from a magazine of a cat that looked slightly like Mrs Mudgely. No note, though. Usually there was a note.

'I will not cry because there is no note from George.' Poppy wiped tears off her cheek. 'Damn! I am not going to get weepy, I've finished with that.' Mrs Mudgely jumped onto her lap and the tears kept coming. 'I'm just tired Mrs M; nothing to worry about. And lonely. Shit!' She scrabbled for the television remote and the gruesome images of a 'don't drink and drive' advertisement vanished into a point in the middle of the screen just before the woman started screaming. The cat was kneading her lap, rubbing against her arm and purring.

Poppy gave up trying to stop crying and let the tears run down her face and drip off her chin. The cat licked her fur where they fell. 'Oh, Mrs M, I know Rose was a mistake, but I miss her anyway. And her sisters and brothers and cousins and aunts and Uncle Tom Cobleigh and all. I wasn't lonely when I could come home and ring Rose and she would come around or I would go to her place and her family would be coming and going and we'd laugh at nothing at all. And her mum would call us her flowers and laugh and say that she didn't know when she named Rose how prickly she would be ...'

The cat looked straight back at Poppy. 'And you don't miss her fights with her sister, and her mother's cigarette smoke and her lecturing you about not going for promotion and having Tupperware meetings in your living room without telling you, never mind asking, and making jokes about you teaching primary school when she got her management job and ...'

'Stop it! Stop it!' Poppy startled herself and the cat by shouting out loud. She must stop putting her thoughts onto Mrs Mudgely. Perhaps she was going mad.

'Or just spending too much time on your own.' The cat turned, kneaded, and settled down on the sofa beside her.

Later, lying in bed with Mrs Mudgely purring at her feet, Poppy gave in to feeling sad and lonely. She had loved being around Rose's family as much as she had loved Rose. None of them kept in touch with her, any more than she did with them. People drifted in and out of that family's orbit and she was sure she would be welcomed if she turned up. But now she wasn't with Rose she didn't have any sense of belonging, she wasn't part of their lives and she didn't know how to be, or even that she wanted to be, on her own. If she baby-sat, ran messages like they all did for each other, hung about and made cups of tea and behaved as though she was part of the family they would accept her, she knew. She didn't feel like one of them, though, she felt like an outsider, an observer, she had only ever been there because she was with Rose. And what if Rose came in with what's-her-name? It was only when she was feeling lonely and bleak that she thought of Rose at all, and then it wasn't really Rose or her family she was lonely for.

When she woke up in the morning, Poppy jumped out of bed, raced through her morning routine and set off for school full of plans for the day. At the door she turned back for the article her father had sent about making painting palettes. Was Mrs M really nodding approvingly at her?

Stuck in traffic on the Harbour Bridge, cursing the unfairness of six of the eight lanes taking traffic the opposite way to her, she ran through the day in her mind; everything had been prepared in the gaps between interviews last night. She was looking forward to being in her classroom, involved with the children, doing what she knew she did well.

The day went quickly, full of reading and writing and maths and playground duty – and joy, when Adam Turnbull had a breakthrough in long division. The class had done some great paintings, mixing their own colours on the newspaper palettes, and as she was admiring them laid out to dry, trying to decide which one she would ask a child for permission to send to George, Amelia came in.

'Hi. Come and look at these, aren't they wonderful?'

'Can we talk?'

'Sure, but look what Shelley has done here with the sky, and Max, who was so excited when he made green himself from yellow and blue, has done this remarkable ... what's up?'

'I want to talk to you, seriously, with you paying attention.'

'Oh, sorry. Come and sit down. What is it?'

There were tears in Amelia's eyes. She wiped them with the tissue Poppy handed her from the box on her desk for children with runny noses.

'Why didn't you come for a drink last night? You know Tony's been hanging around me, and, well, we were the only two who went to the pub in the end.'

'I thought you liked Tony "hanging around" as you say. I thought you said you rather fancied him.'

'Well, yes, but we were the only ones there and we had a few wines and one thing led to another, you know.'

Poppy tried not to laugh. 'Where did you go?'

'My sister's – she's still away and I've got the key to water her plants. And – please don't laugh – we both fell asleep afterwards. Ian was frantic when I rang him at five this morning, and he'd already rung Moana at home, and he said Jason had woken in the night and wanted me – oh, my poor baby! – and I rushed out while Tony was ringing his wife so I don't know what he said to her, and I have had to tell all these lies, and I said you were with us, you won't let me down, will you?'

'Oh, Amelia, what a mess! It's not fair getting me mixed up in your drama, and I certainly don't like being dropped in it.' Poppy was determined not to laugh; getting angry with Amelia made that easier. 'But I suppose I can just keep quiet. Whatever were you thinking of? Why didn't you at least plan it and set up your lies in advance? Was the sex good, was it worth it?'

'You are a very good friend to me Poppy, but sometimes your direct way of talking is hard to deal with. You make me feel dishonest. If you had been there at the pub it wouldn't have happened!'

'Hold on a minute, I'm not taking the blame. You and Tony are both grown-up people – I suppose – and you could have gone straight home yourself, you know. You'd better tell me your story, if I'm to, reluctantly mind you, be an accessory. Shit Amelia! I hate lies and I'm no good at them, I'm bound to get something wrong. What did Tony tell his wife? Am I implicated in that too? And you didn't answer my other question.'

'I don't know what Tony said.' Amelia's voice rose higher with every word. 'I haven't been able to speak to him all day and Moana bailed me up at lunchtime and said she didn't know what was going on and didn't want to but as principal of the school, blah blah blah, you know the kind of thing.'

'Well, you'd better tell me what your story was.'

'Thank you, Poppy, you're such a good friend.' Poppy turned away, not sure by now whether she was really annoyed or more amused. 'I told Ian that you and I and a couple of other teachers went to the bar near my sister's after parent interviews and we all had too much to drink to drive home, and you know how expensive it is to get a cab over the bridge, and we walked to my sister's and crashed there and I was quite tiddly and fell asleep before I thought to ring him. It's pretty feeble and he's really angry because he worried all night and of course he never thought to ring my sister's because he knows she's away ...'

The headline and Mrs Mudgely's grinning face appeared where the wall joined the ceiling at about the same time. 'Teacher mother in post-parent-interview sinfest with young colleague.'

'Go away,' instructed Poppy, sotto voce.

'What?'

'Nothing. Okay, I'll go along with your story but if anyone asks me a straight question I won't add any more lies, I'm no good at them and I'll forget what I said to whom. Hadn't you better find out what Tony's story is? And was the sex worth it? You still haven't said.'

'You are awful.' Amelia smiled coyly, looking at her hands in her lap. 'Well yes, it was actually, it was wonderful. Younger men have so much more, well, um, energy, I suppose.'

'So poor old Ian's getting past it, is he? At what, forty-five?'

'Stop it, Poppy, you're not fair, and it's not just sex, I think I'm in love.' When there was no response to this announcement, Amelia continued, 'I haven't talked to Tony since this morning. I came over here because I saw Moana going into his room and, well, I didn't know what for, and I must pick up Jason and get home before Ian and …' Her voice turned into a wail, 'What am I going to do?'

'Well, to start with, you can talk to Tony; he's coming over here right now.'

Amelia blushed, giggled, and stood up, turning her back to the door and looking beseechingly at Poppy. 'Please be kind to me.'

Poppy choked. She was saved from answering by Tony's entrance. He was not his usual bouncy self. His, 'Hi, Poppy,' was subdued.

'Hi, Tony. This is a right mess. Did you implicate me in your story as well? Am I to perjure myself to your wife, to Moana and god knows who else?'

'What? I didn't implicate you in anything. I told my wife I got drunk at school after the interviews and crashed in the staffroom. She didn't really care. We pretty much go our own way these days. She said it was just as well she hadn't wanted to go out as it would have been hard to get a baby-sitter at such short notice and would I make a point of being in tonight, as she was going – I forget – somewhere.' The words came out fast. Tony was not looking at Poppy. He moved towards Amelia, who was still facing the wall, hesitated and glanced at Poppy.

'Feel free,' she said, 'to use my classroom, but please don't fornicate in it. I'm off. See you both on Monday.'

As she got into her car she saw Moana waving at her from the office. She waved back, calling out, 'Bye, have a good weekend,' and drove off.

Was she really a such good friend to Amelia, she wondered. Would Amelia be so sure about her friendship if she knew how silly Poppy thought her a lot of the time; a forty-something teenager married to an eye surgeon, big house, flash car, entertaining the mayor, and now fooling around with a colleague at least ten years younger than her and also married? She was a good teacher, though, she understood children, and had managed to turn around some of the more difficult six-year-olds. Good colleague, silly woman, Poppy concluded. Then she heard an echo of Rose, 'There you go again, you've got to put everyone in a pigeon-hole, categorise them, instead of just taking them – me – as I am.'

Friday evenings, between the end of the working day and darkness, were when Poppy most often felt lonely. The world was heading into its coupled and familied nests it seemed to her, everyone else with someone to meet or go home to without having to make an arrangement. She often met a friend for dinner out on a Friday, but today she had intended to stay at school late and make a wall display from the paintings, as well as writing up her planning for the coming week, in advance for once, and maybe even having a chat with Moana if she was around, about some ideas she had for Year Four maths. How had she let Amelia and Tony take over her room and her plans? She felt loose-endish, crotchety, out of sorts and couldn't decide what to do. Who could she ring at the last moment? Martia? Jan and Ruth? Rina? Felicity? Eve? Nah, she was too crabby for company.

Her mailbox was overflowing and it was all junk mail. Gathering a handful of colourful brochures, she realised she hadn't cleared her email for three days, and also she was hungry, really hungry. Dumping the mail in the bin, giving Mrs M a quick 'hello' and pat and surveying the contents of the fridge were all she did before heading back out to the supermarket.

The crowded carpark and empty trolley bay reminded her why she hardly ever did this on a Friday but she persisted, grabbing a newly abandoned trolley before it came to a stop and setting off with fierce determination in search of a smoked chicken, maybe, or steak – no, not at that price – the makings of a salad, fruit, chocolate – no – icecream – yes – did she need washing-up liquid? It took longer to get to the front of the checkout queue than it had to load her trolley and, by the time she had the bags of shopping in the boot of her car, her bad temper had worsened.

Shaking olive oil, garlic, mustard, and balsamic vinegar in a jar, and watching, from her kitchen window, the petals drop from a daffodil under the big magnolia tree on the back border of her garden, Poppy felt herself relaxing again. A generous portion of chicken was arranged on a plate, a potato was circling in the microwave, and Mrs Mudgely was on a promise of soft chicken bones. She could handle being on her own, enjoy it even, she told herself. Hell, at forty-seven she certainly should be able to, and she'd been alone before. 'And lonely and miserable. Why do you think you were enchanted by Rose?' The words rose out of the purring at her ankles.

Three, no, four, if she counted those two days in London in 'seventy-six, four relationships she had had over the years since that first tortuous heartbreak at seventeen. All of them had been happy, at least some of the time, and she regretted none, except perhaps the London incident. Four relationships, including thirteen years with Kate.

As always, everything froze and she felt the absolute stillness that took over whenever thoughts of Kate crept up on her. No petals fell from the daffodil, no breeze shifted the leaves of the magnolia. The clouds were motionless. She had no thoughts, no feelings. There was no time.

'Damn!' Poppy licked at the salad dressing that was running down her arm and finished assembling her meal. 'French bread and potato and to hell with the consequences,' she announced to Mrs Mudgely, heading with a loaded plate for the chair that had the best view of the television.

Two unmemorable programmes later she remembered she had been going to check her email. 'Sorry, puss, you have the seat to yourself for a bit. I guess you won't care if I turn this off.'

The office and computer room doubled as an extra spare bedroom. The real spare bedroom was just big enough for a double bed and a set of drawers and got the morning sun as well as a view up the slopes of Maungawhau, the best in the house. When she had first moved in Poppy considered it for herself, but chose her big front room where she didn't see the hill at all but looked over the suburbs to the west and could watch the sunsets, and now would not change. While she waited for her iMac to boot up, she flicked through the pages about chat rooms she had printed out last time she had ventured onto the world-wide-web. Maybe she should join one, and have some nice, safe, distant, human contact. Maybe.

She scanned her fifteen messages. Several from mac-women, bound to be helpful and technical, she'd look at them later. She read the ones from Sara in Christchurch and Mel in Te Atatu, both full of news of her friends' doings and enquiring after hers, leaving the one from the father until last. She skimmed down it – he was about to go on another field trip for the museum, to the Lake District, looking for his beloved trichoptera, as well as the lepidoptera that were one of the museum's special collections. As a volunteer at the museum he seemed to do as much, seven years after he had retired, as when he was paid a salary; as good a way to retire as any for someone who didn't like change, Poppy supposed. Susanna's arthritis was worse, so she probably wouldn't go; the weather had been awful with rain every day; there was yet another controversy around one of the chemical factories at nearby Billingham; and then,

You will have received the package I sent by now. I included two photographs of myself and some of my colleagues here at the museum. They still treat me as a colleague you know, I appreciate that, and the working space they let me have. We had a chap from London here last week, and he was impressed by our insects, 'the best regional collection I've seen,' he said and I must say I was chuffed. Anyway, one of my colleagues Jane Blackie is coming to New Zealand soon ...

Poppy felt her stomach sink. The father had 'sent' her people from England before. Most of them had lives so different from her own that she had to work hard with them, and they never made the same effort with her, assuming their concerns were hers.

... Jane (she's the one on the left in the photos) is our Exhibitions Curator here at the museum and a bequest means there is a small amount of money for her to travel to New Zealand and see for herself

the developments at Auckland and at the national museum in Wellington. This is not an expensive junket I am afraid, we are such small fry in the museum world here, but she has an air fare and some money for expenses. At the moment she is thinking of going to New Zealand in the first week of December, doing her work for three weeks and staying on, at her own expense of course, until the middle of January. I did point out to her that she would see in the new millennium, even though we all know it is nonsense, before any of the rest of us here. She's a reserved person, I don't think I have ever had a conversation about anything personal with her, but very pleasant. I did wonder if you had made holiday plans yet. Well, that is up to you. I have given her your email address, but she seems rather shy of writing to you, so perhaps you could contact her. I'll put her address at the end of this message.

'How dare you! How dare you! How dare you interfere in my life!' She was startled by her own anger. 'You have no right to give people my address! You are a stupid, fusspot, interfering old man. I am a grown woman, nearly fifty, when will you stop trying to organise my life?' Poppy realised she was stroking Mrs Mudgely a lot more fiercely than usual. 'It's all right, Mrs M, I know he's a dear really, don't look at me like that. I am just too tired to be looking out for an up-tight English curator, and I certainly don't want to take her camping with me at Christmas, I am going to do that by myself.'

Scratching between the ears restored the cat's relaxed purring once the shouting stopped.

'The last time I went camping with anyone was with Kate. It's the one thing I have never wanted to do with anyone else.'

2

1977

Poppy had taught for three years after she finished at the Teacher's Training College, and then, in 1975, set off overseas. She stumbled across women's liberation writings in her travels and found that reading them made her feel guilty; what she read about violence against women and children and pornography and race and class and injustice generally made her feel guilty for her easy life and she felt she should be doing something about all of them. Then it would be time to move on to the next new city, new country, new culture and the guilt would dissipate. Her friend Martia sent her a copy of a magazine, *Circle*, that lesbians in Wellington published and she found that particularly hard to read; she knew some of the women writing in it and they were so ... so ... exposed, there on the pages in black and white. Published writing, in Poppy's experience, was produced by people you didn't know who lived in countries other than hers, and she had never been aware that there was anything she needed liberating from.

She returned to Auckland in January 1977, moved into a large house in Grafton Road with four other women, and got a teaching job in Mangere.

'You'll need a car for all that travelling to work,' announced Katrina, and lent her two thousand dollars to buy one.

'I'll come looking with you,' offered Stefan. 'I bet you know nothing at all about cars.' Stefan was into being responsible, now he was soon to be a father; May-Yun was eight months pregnant. Poppy was a mixture of pleased and embarrassed when May-Yun placed her hand onto her swollen belly and said, 'Say hello to aunty, little one.'

There was something reassuring about her New Zealand family's pragmatic response to her return; it was very different from her father's tears when she had left London. She believed they loved her, and only occasionally wished they would show more affection. And she loved them, in an 'of course', taking-it-for-granted way.

Her parents had been Katrina and George Sinclair, married couple of Westmere, Auckland. George the entomologist, who was happiest when he was seeking, researching or classifying trichoptera, had been a fond, slightly distracted father, who took Poppy with him to streams and eddies all around the city. Katrina, an accountant in the public service, prided herself on her 'well-cared-for children', now and then playfully whisking them off to a park or zoo or the pictures or a picnic with a rush and huge exuberance. 'Come on, lovelies, let's all go and have an adventure,' she would say, and away they would all go, George usually taking a net and a jar, 'just in case'. He would drive and Katrina would turn in her seat, talking and laughing with Poppy and Stefan in the back, playing games like counting cars of different colours. (Stefan always chose white and always got to twenty first.) Other times Katrina was busy.

Poppy and Stefan hardly fought. They hardly did anything together. 'Different temperaments,' said George. 'Like Katrina and me, not much in common, but we get along all right, don't we girl?' And they did. Mum-and-Dad had been the foundation of her world, both utterly dependable and predictable (even Katrina's 'adventures' were predictable – there would often be signs of one approaching the night before). Poppy liked it like that. Both her parents always took the same position on going out and who she could stay overnight with, she could never go to the other if she had been told 'no' by one of them. Her life as a child was sheltered, trauma-free, and, in her mind, ordinary.

Even when all the girls around her were obsessed about boys she was never excited by them. She liked having a boyfriend best when she was eleven and twelve, and the point of the boyfriend was to talk to your girlfriends about him.

'D'you think he likes me?'

'Yeah. He rode his bike right up on the footpath when he went past.'

'Did he look? My hair's awful.'

'He looked like he wanted to talk to you but you were looking at the ground.'

'Did he? Did he really? Let's go to my place and I'll get changed out of this yuk uniform and we can walk to your place; he lives in the next street to you.'

'How do you know that.'

'I dunno, I just do.'

Mrs Greenhalgh was her first real crush, starting in the fourth form. Poppy obsessed about her for two years, imagining a new disaster or tragedy each week, where she, Poppy, rescued/comforted the Geography teacher, who was so grateful they became best friends. Every fantasy had an ending, a vague, beautiful ending, with Mrs Greenhalgh – Marina – the most beautiful name in the world – holding Poppy, stroking her hair and gazing into her eyes. After that there would be a radiant, golden haze that carried them both away to some glorious, undefined hereafter.

Poppy had been in her middle year at Teachers' College when her parents separated. At first she'd refused to believe they meant it. Stefan had said, 'Grow up, Poppy. For heaven's sake, you're going to be a school teacher soon, don't be such a baby, they've been miserable together for years. Politely miserable.'

'Stefan! No! We were happy, they were happy.'

'Maybe, at first. You always lived in your own world, you wouldn't have noticed anything that didn't fit your rosy view, making the best of everything, pretending we were all happy together those Sundays when Mum was trying so hard and Dad was looking out for a stream so he could go off and hunt insects. I guess caddis flies didn't think of him as lazy and unambitious.'

'Stefan, I never knew you ...' He brushed her hand off his arm.

'It's in the past now, there's no point in raking over it all. Dad's happy with Susanna and Mum's happy making money, so get over it, and get on with your own life.'

'Stefan ...'

'Gotta go, meeting someone. 'Bye sis.'

Later that year she fell in love with Irene, another trainee teacher. They partied, made love, shared a seedy flat, were late with assignments, late to class, and got drunk blushingly often. When Irene dropped out of TC they drifted. Poppy came home one day and Irene wasn't there and she was relieved. The experiment with a man 'in case I am not really a – um – lesbian' was not a success. 'I guess I am'.

She told her parents, who were nicely liberal about it. George made his first reference in years to his older brother, Gregory in Sydney, saying he was, 'probably gay, but we've never talked about it.' Then he gave her a hug and said she would always be his 'dearest girl' and never raised it again. Two months later he left for England with Susanna. He asked after her 'friends' in his letters and remembered every name she mentioned in hers.

Katrina was brisk.

'It's your life, Penelope ('Mu – um, Poppy is fine'), and just as well I am not sitting around waiting for grandchildren. Be happy, dear, that's the main thing.' And she was off.

Stefan grunted, 'I thought as much. Runs in the family I guess. Thank heavens I'm normal.'

17

Living in the house in Grafton Road was tiring. There were meetings in the living room several nights a week, with a 'consciousness-raising group' on Tuesdays when she and the two others not in the group were expected to be either out or very unobtrusive. Poppy didn't take part in any of the meetings, though she was often invited to 'come along if you want to'. They could be noisy, with a lot of laughing, occasionally shouting. She started reading some of the papers lying about: pamphlets on abortion, fact sheets on domestic violence, announcements of meetings about 'lesbian visibility in the women's movement', an occasional copy of *Broadsheet*. None of it felt connected to her. She liked the other women in the house, mostly, but they alarmed her with their intensity, their energy, their frank sexual conversations, their urgency. She retreated to her room quite often, which didn't mean, she realised, that she was unhappy living there. In fact, she liked it. She had never minded being on the edge of things.

Leanne, who Poppy thought of as in charge of house matters, though no-one ever said so, called a house meeting and she and a couple of the others said they were lesbian separatists and wanted the house to be a women-only space. Which meant that men could not come in. Boys would be okay if they were under twelve and with their mothers. Poppy was shocked. She didn't know what to think. As she never had visitors to the house anyway, except for Martia occasionally, she didn't think it mattered to her so she nodded and agreed where necessary.

That was the night she decided she would have to do some serious reading. She asked Eve, who she felt easiest with, for some ideas. Eve wrote her a list, and lent her *Of Woman Born*, by Adrienne Rich, which a friend had sent from America and she had just finished. Leanne dropped *Lesbian Nation* off at her room, saying, 'Eve says you want stuff to read,' and she saw Simone de Beauvoir's *The Second Sex* in a bookshop in Queen Street and it was on Eve's list, so she bought it.

As she read, she saw her mother's busy-ness in a different light. She wanted to tell May-Yun about Adrienne Rich and realised that they only saw each other when Stefan was around, and she couldn't talk to him about these ideas, not yet, anyway. Reading Jill Johnston in *Lesbian Nation* made sense of the women in the house, why they were fired up with zeal to change the world, to 'overthrow the patriarchy' – a phrase she couldn't even think of without looking around to see if anyone was noticing.

Poppy left Simone de Beauvoir until last, because that was the one she didn't have to give back to anyone. She was glad she did, it was far and away the longest and the hardest. It was difficult to concentrate in the evenings, after a day's teaching. She persisted, though, and spent one whole wet Sunday in bed with Simone.

It was that Sunday, late in the afternoon, when she emerged looking for food, that she overheard Eve and another woman she didn't know talking about how to get someone to the airport that night. As she made a peanut butter sandwich she realised they were arranging for a woman to go to Sydney for an abortion. 'I can take her,' she said, 'I'd like to help.'

She never knew the woman's name. She was older than Poppy had expected, possibly even forty, and wore a wedding ring. 'Five children already, bastard of a husband,' was all Eve told her. The woman didn't speak all the way to the airport. She smiled at Poppy and said, 'Thank you,' so quietly Poppy hardly heard as she got out of the car with Eve. Poppy said she'd wait in the car park. There were to be many more such trips, and Eve and Poppy would become friends on the drives back to Grafton Road. Poppy found out that she hated meetings and trying to organise other people, but she felt really good about doing the airport runs. Some women she took to their flight and also met off the return journey. They never talked much and she never minded that.

In April someone moved out of the house and Kate moved in. By this time Poppy was staying around for more of the conversations that seemed to her like arguments, though people were mostly still friends afterwards. Some were about being separatist, and how to carry that out. Where did fathers, brothers, sons, gay men fit into their lives, or didn't they at all? One woman cut off from her family completely. Monogamy and how they had to create new relationships based on new values, not the ownership of one person (woman) by another (man) was often discussed. As lesbians they must show the world how it was possible for women to be non-monogamous was one argument, how sexual jealousy was a tool of the patriarchy, designed to keep women subservient. Poppy knew there were lots of sexual relationships formed and unformed among women in the house, often with more than one woman at a time. She felt very conservative and unadventurous but was relieved they simply accepted, she supposed, that she was not part of that, and left her alone.

Everyone else had stories about violence or emotional or sexual abuse in their families. Eve asked Poppy once what had happened to her in her family and Poppy replied, 'Nothing.' And it was true. She thought about it later and it was true. The parents separating was awful, but they didn't row, they explained it all to Poppy and Stefan almost apologetically, being painstakingly adult and respectful with them and with each other. As for George being a representative of the patriarchy, Poppy couldn't see her father in that light at all; had Katrina been a man, she would have embodied the concept much more closely.

Poppy hardly noticed Kate at first. She was tall and athletic-looking and rapidly became part of the crowd.

'Hey, you're a teacher, Leanne tells me. I'm a nurse. How's that for a couple of good, stereotypical jobs for girls, oops, women.'

Poppy started and looked up from the banana cake she was mixing.

'Yeah. I suppose. And look what I'm doing now. I'm not much of a revolutionary, I guess.' Eyes, Kate had eyes the colour of the mangroves in the mud-flats around Westmere in the setting sun, and hair the same brown, cut short. Blushing when she realised she was staring, Poppy stirred vigorously.

'I've got no problem with anyone who bakes cakes.' And Kate scooped out a finger-full of mixture. 'Yum, are there plans for this cake?'

'Cook it, cool it and add lemon icing.'

'Uh, I was thinking more of the eating phase, really. Unless you're actually the little red hen.'

'Oh. No, of course I'm not. It's for Eve's new group she's starting tonight, for women who think they might be lesbian. It's the first night, and she was wondering how to welcome them, 'cos the room at the Y is a bit bleak, so I suggested flowers and a cake and I would make the cake.'

'Damn, I don't think I qualify for a coming out group. Maybe I could regress.'

Poppy looked straight at her. 'You're teasing me.' And smiled.

'Yes, I am. You should smile more often, that's a great smile.'

'Um, are you flirting now?'

'Whew, that's direct! Yes, I guess I am. Flirting, that is. When the cake's done how about a walk up to the domain, there could be a good sunset.'

'Uh, I've got to get ready for school tomorrow, you know, thirty nine-year-olds to teach.'

'Sure thing. Well, nice to have a chat anyway. See ya.'

Exactly forty-eight hours later Poppy knocked on Kate's door. 'It looks like another good sunset, would you like …?'

'Sure would.'

That evening they walked until dark and talked until midnight then went to their separate rooms. The next night Poppy had a staff meeting after school and dinner at Stefan and May-Yun's arranged. The night after that Kate was working a shift at the hospital until eleven. Poppy decided not to wait up for her to come in and then had trouble getting to sleep even after she had heard the front door, the

21

bathroom door and Kate's door. Just in case she had got it wrong she opened her door a crack and peeped, and sure enough there was a light under Kate's. Should she … the light went out, so she went back to bed to not sleep some more. Why hadn't she thought to leave her light on, then Kate might have come over?

On Friday evening, as Poppy was going in the front door after dinner with Martia, Kate came out.

'Hi Poppy. I really enjoyed watching the sunset with you. Want to try a sunrise with me tomorrow? I'm going sailing early.'

'Sailing?'

'Yes. You know, on the water. I've got a twelve-footer. I sail it by myself a lot but it can take two. Have you ever sailed?'

'No, just been out in a rowing dinghy. And on the ferry to Devonport, of course, and Waiheki.' Poppy moved her weight from one foot to the other; she knew she sounded like an idiot.

'It's not hard, just so long as you duck when the boom slides over. And it is the most wonderful, thrilling thing, to be on the water!' Kate stopped, looking embarrassed at her own enthusiasm. 'Anyways, I'm leaving at six and I'll be back by one. If you want to come I'll see you at the tea pot just before six. Hey, I'm off to the KG club now, d'you want to come?' Poppy shook her head. Kate looked at her for a moment. 'Bye then, see you,' and was off.

'Why not?' thought Poppy, still standing on the step. 'Why not go with her? Because you are scared,' she answered herself, 'scared to get mixed up with such a –a – a – a – feminist, that's what, scared that you won't be good enough, scared that she'll be disappointed in you, scared she'll find you boring, just plain damn scared.'

In the morning Poppy couldn't decide what to wear. Not jeans, they were too heavy if they got wet. Shorts, then, a t-shirt. Cap. Sun block, there was nothing attractive about a peeling nose. ('Why am I thinking about being attractive, I'm going sailing, for heaven's sake?') A jacket? She stuffed her blue-and-black-checked Swanny into a duffel bag and added a long-sleeved shirt. Ten to six.

'Well, hi. I wasn't sure you'd come. Cuppa?'

'Thanks. Neither was I. Sure, that is. But here I am.'

'Great. Well, drink up and let's go. I usually grab a sandwich from the corner shop in Bayswater, if that's okay with you.'

'Yes. Sure. Um, do you want to take my car?'

'No, it's okay, I know where we're going.' Kate stopped and grinned at Poppy. 'We'll take yours next time.'

On the drive Kate explained that her boat was at her parents' house. They lived out at Bayswater Point and she could only get it in and out of the water three hours either side of high tide, which dictated the times she could go sailing.

'If I don't get out every week during summer I get crotchety. It's a wonderful antidote to working in the hospital system, nodding and scraping to doctors who know diddley-sqat. That's what made me a feminist, you know, being a nurse.'

'I don't understand'.

'The whole hospital system is so sexist. The doctors think they are gods and expect the nurses to treat them as if they are. And lots of us do. Not me, not now. It's just as well I'm not ambitious.'

'Oh.' Poppy couldn't see any connection between feminism and not being ambitious. And it was her turn to say something. 'I don't know if I'm a feminist,' she blurted, 'I'm reading *The Second Sex* and it certainly makes sense of things. But I hate meetings and arguments.'

'You don't have to go to meetings to be a feminist.' Poppy was relieved when Kate chipped in and then continued, 'You just have to see the world how it really is, how women get the short straw, every time: we get paid less, we're the victims of domestic violence, we do all the housework and childcare, we become "just a housewife" … Sorry, I didn't mean to give you a lecture.' Poppy glanced at her, and quickly away again; she didn't look or sound sorry.

'No, you're not lecturing me.' She managed, and pushed determinedly on. 'What about –um – lesbians?'

'What about us? We're the best! You are, aren't you?'

'Oh, yes. But I don't make much of it, I'm a teacher you see, and people seem to think …'.

'Yep, they do. Only nice, normal heterosexuals for our children, please. And, ooooh, stay away from our wives. Makes me sick. Here's the sandwich place.'

'Let me get them.' Poppy was relieved she didn't have to find a response to such, well, strong support. 'What do you like?'

'Ham and mustard, and cheese and onion. You get hungry out on the water.'

Kate's parents' place was large and right at the water's edge. The kitchen was all stainless steel. Her father was drinking coffee and reading the paper in the dining room. He glanced up, not taking his attention fully from the paper. 'Your mother's not up yet, won't be for hours, I've got to go in to the office this morning.'

'Hi Dad, this is Poppy. We're going sailing.' Kate touched his arm and he patted her hand.

'Hello. Mr …' Poppy realised she didn't know Kate's last name.

'Call me Bob. Nice day for it,' and he went back to his paper.

'Smith,' said Kate, leading the way out the back door. 'I'm Kate Smith. Mum hates it.'

Poppy discovered that she hated sailing. It was really hard work, especially dealing with the boat before and after being on the water. And when they were sailing she never knew when the boom was going to swing around, and she felt inept and clumsy and was either too hot or too cold most of the time. She could only eat one sandwich and that got splashed and soggy before she had finished it. Sure, the harbour was beautiful and the big keelers gliding past were even more elegant close up than they were from the Harbour Bridge, but she felt miserable on the water. Kate, on the other hand gave new meaning to the saying 'in her element'. She sparkled as brightly as the water, was smooth as well as exuberant in her movements, and knew exactly when to duck. She stacked out, pulled ropes – 'They're called sheets, actually,' – and laughed when waves splashed her, all with one hand on the tiller.

'D'you want to have a go?'

'Okay.' Maybe if she was doing something it would be better. Poppy clambered to the back of the boat and grasped the tiller tightly. It was, in fact, just more scary. The wind was light, but still the pull on the rudder was stronger than she had expected. She was relieved when Kate said, 'I'd better take it now. I think the wind is dying and if we don't get back in soon we'll be stuck out here all day. And I'm on afternoon duty.' Kate grinned at her, a great big, wide, happy grin. 'Here, hold this while we change places.' Poppy didn't grasp the rope firmly enough and the mains'l flapped and the boom swung wildly. Poppy let go the rope completely and dived into the bottom of the boat. Kate grabbed it, sat on the aft transom, and pulled the tiller around and the sail in, all in one smooth movement.

'Sorry.'

'It's okay. If there had been a decent blow we would both have ended up in the water.' And Kate looked as though she would have enjoyed that.

Poppy was relieved when they had the boat in, the sails folded, the mast down, the centre-board stowed. Kate's mother was in the kitchen now, Bob presumably gone to the office. 'Hello Mrs Smith, I'm Poppy.' Kate's mother waved her hand in the direction of Poppy's tentatively proffered handshake. Her housecoat was shiny satin, pale pink.

'Call me Belinda, dear. Will you girls stay for lunch?' Kate offered Poppy a glass of orange juice, which she drank straight down. She hadn't noticed before how thirsty she was.

'No thanks, Mum, I'm on afternoon duty.'

'Oh. All right then, dear.' Mrs Smith's disappointment was palpable. 'I'll go and have my shower then.'

'Too much money and not enough to do,' said Kate as they got in the car.

'What?'

'My mother.'

'She looked sad.'

'Don't. I get impatient with her and feel bad enough without other people being sorry for her. She's never been any more than Mrs Bob Smith since she married Dad and it's such a waste. She used to be funny, you know, and she could sing. Dad didn't like it, thought it cheapened her. Now she just drinks too much. Bloody men.'

'I'm sorry.'

'Don't be. She's well off in her misery, nice house, credit card, all that. Not like some of the women who come into the hospital.'

Back at the house, Poppy thanked Kate, who said, 'It was a pleasure,' with at least one eyebrow raised. 'I've got to get ready for work, I guess. I hate afternoon shift on Saturdays. I suppose you're going out on the town.'

'Well, actually, I'm going to do some work for school. Um, when you come in, you know, after work, would you like to come to my room for a cuppa?'

'I had rather hoped for champagne and caviar.'

'I don't have either of those in at the moment,' Poppy's voice was tight, 'but I do have a jug.'

'Oops, sorry, no teasing allowed. A cup of tea will be great. I'll look forward to it. I'll get away as quickly as I can and see you soon after eleven.' With a wave and a grin, Kate was gone.

Poppy did most of the school preparation she had planned before she tidied her room, re-arranged it twice, brought a tray in from the kitchen with mugs, milk and sugar, got out her packet of chocolate biscuits, put them away, got them out again. She sat on the edge of her bed, feeling like the most uninteresting, wimpish twenty-four-year-old lesbian in the world. When she heard the front door close she peeked out the window and checked that Kate's car was indeed parked outside. Its headlights were still on.

There was a tap on the door and Kate's head appeared.

'Hi there, expecting anyone?'

'Uh-huh. Um, you've left your headlights on.'

'You peeped! Don't go away, I'll be right back.'

Poppy turned the jug on again, knocked a cup off the table and caught it before it hit the floor.

'Thanks. I'm glad you noticed my lights, I'd have had a rotten flat battery in the morning if you hadn't. I'm usually really careful about turning them off, I must have been distracted.'

Poppy couldn't think what to say so she didn't say anything. A fist of misery clutched at her stomach. She gestured towards the armchair by the window. She could not look at Kate.

'Thanks.' Kate slouched into it and looked at Poppy for a moment. 'You don't much like being teased, do you?'

'No. My brother teased me a lot and I never could tell the difference between it and, you know, ordinary talking.' Poppy gave herself a shake and turned to look determinedly into Kate's eyes. 'And I'm no good at flirting either, I can never tell until afterwards what was going on and feel stupid for not getting it and it seems dishonest somehow, even though I know that often people are just having fun, it doesn't mean anything. Anyhow, I get terribly confused.' Her words faded away but she held her gaze. 'If I try and play those games I get really, really miserable, and I know everyone here thinks I'm prudish and boring, but it's just the way I am and you don't have to stay if you don't want to. Sorry.' Her eyes dropped.

'Hey, I want to stay. How about that cuppa I was promised, I'm parched.' Kate got up from the chair, and as Poppy turned to the shelf with the jug and cups, sat on the edge of the bed. 'Look, the women in the house don't think what you think they think about you. If you see what I mean. They find you reserved, sure, but they like your directness, and that you pitch in when there's something to be done …' Now Kate's voice faded away, as Poppy turned around, proffering a mug. 'Milk? Sugar?'

'Just milk, thanks. Please come and sit down,' she patted the bed beside her. 'That's rich, I'm inviting you to sit on your own bed.'

They sat side by side sipping tea. Kate spoke first. 'Poppy, I like you a lot, even though you'll never be a sailor. Oh, I'm sorry, that's a tease, I just do it, I can't help it. It helps, you know, keep things in perspective. Like I said, I like you a lot, there's something, well, true about you, and you don't hide things. You looked so-o-o miserable on the water this morning. If that had been me, I would have put on such a show of loving it. Look at me, Poppy, say something.'

First Poppy put her mug on the floor. Then she turned and looked at Kate. 'I like you too. And I feel like a gawky teenager around you, all clunky and gauche. Maybe we should work on just being friends for a while.'

'Is that what you want?'

'No'.

Kate leaned forward and kissed her on the mouth, briefly. 'I have been wanting to do that since the first time I saw you smile, over the cake dough.' Poppy looked back at her, eyes wide open, then giggled. 'A friend of mine,' she said, 'told me that the first time she kissed a woman she felt like a fruit machine, you know, when all the pictures come up in a line and the bells and whistles go berserk. Now I know what she was talking about.' And she kissed Kate back, and then it wasn't clear who was kissing and who was being kissed; the world was one kiss that went on and on. Then they were on the bed, clothes, watches, rings flying.

Kate went on teasing and Poppy went on being prickly about it. Three months later they moved from the Grafton Road house to a flat in Grey Lynn on their own. Leanne said to Poppy that she was brassed off at losing two flat mates who paid their share of the rent and the bills on time, and added, 'I never took Kate for the marrying kind. I've always thought of her as a good-time girl who likes a party, especially when there's whisky, and never mind going home with one you came with – so to speak.'

What Leanne was saying made no sense to Poppy so she ignored it. 'I still want to help with the run to the airport,' she said, 'I'll let you know the number when we get the phone connected.'

'Cheers, see ya.'

3

1999

Dear George,

Yes, I got the package, thank you. And the cutting about the art classes had in it a very good idea about newspaper palettes for children's painting which I have used and I am sending you one of the paintings. Yvonne, who painted it, was thrilled that it was going to England!

I haven't contacted the woman, Jane, nor she me. I'm rather visited-out at present, actually.

Sorry to hear about Susanna's arthritis. Give her my love.

We just had another round of parent interviews at school. I still hate them. The whole set-up is so artificial. I guess plenty of parents can't come to school during the day, but I'm going to figure out a different way to do it for next year; the ten-minute interview is diabolical.

Two of the teachers at school started having an affair on the same night as the interviews. One of them is Amelia, who you met last time you were here. It's like a soap opera and I am trying very hard not to be a bit player in it – Amelia has already used me as an alibi once.

She couldn't think of any more to say. The bit about the woman was feeble, but she hated hurting George's feelings, so she signed off with her usual, *love, Poppy* and sent it off. While she waited for the modem to connect she picked up Mrs Mudgely and rubbed her face in the cat's fur. The end-of-year blahs were coming on early, she thought, it was only just October.

Her new mail included an invitation from Mel to a pot-luck at the weekend. Mrs M gave a cat grunt as she put her down to enter the pot-luck in her diary. 'Yes, my dear Mrs Mudgely, there is a limit to my anti-socialness.' Oh. Poppy stared at the name in the 'who' column of her inbox. The theme music for Shortland Street started, so she decided that jane.blackie@clevelandmuseum could wait for a bit and went to watch it, Mrs Mudgely close at her heels, ready for a settled half-hour of stroking and cuddles.

Martia rang as the programme finished. 'Hello stranger, I thought I'd better ring and make sure we haven't fallen out, it's been so long.'

'No, of course we haven't. And there are two ends to a phone, you know. I've not been very sociable lately, busy at school, you know how it is …'

'… years starting to tell on you are they? They are on me, that's for sure, this new job is wearing me out.'

'But Martia, it's only twenty hours …'

'And? I'm still doing two call-out shifts a week as well as the office admin. job – it's the first time in twenty years I've been paid for Rape Crisis work, you know – and I'm on the national collective as well as the local one and visiting Mum every second day and I do all the housework and washing here in return for a lower rent, so just mind what you say about only twenty hours.'

'Sorry. You're right, I wasn't thinking of all those other things. And I've rather got the blahs. How is your mother?'

'Old, frail, stubborn about staying in her place, which I can't say I blame her for. But it's hard. When I suggested a cleaner for the kitchen and bathroom she said, "There's no need for that dear, you do it when you come." Which I do and resent. But I left that for next time. What have you been up to? And what's this about blahs?'

'The father has threatened to send me another visitor from England. I've just got an email from her.'

'They can only get better after the last one. What does she say?'

'I don't know, I haven't read it yet.'

'Well, go on. Read it to me.'

'Okay. I'll have to shift Mrs M and go into the other room.'

'Still ruled by the cat, huh.'

'Ha. She's the one that depends on me for food. Here we are. I'll read it to you.'

Dear Ms Sinclair,

'Crikey, that's a bit formal.'

'Just be quiet and let me read.'

You do not know me, I am a colleague of your father's at the Cleveland Museum of Natural History. He gave me your address and I hope you do not mind me writing to you. George insisted that I should. He may have told you that I am coming to New Zealand in about five weeks to study developments at your museums in Auckland and Wellington, as we are soon to embark on a re-development programme here. I have a small budget for the trip and George suggested you might be able to give me some tips on economical places to stay. I will have nearly a month in Auckland followed by two weeks in Wellington. After that, I am taking a few weeks' annual leave to see something of New Zealand, at my own expense of course. I am a birdwatcher, with a special interest in sea-birds, and a hiker and would appreciate any tips you could give me about ways to see some of your country, which George tells me is very beautiful, and indulge in my interests fairly inexpensively. I have brochures from a travel agent for some rather expensive bus tours and am hoping there are alternatives. I do prefer to be an independent traveller.

Again, please do not go to any trouble, and I would be glad of any information. Thank you.

Jane Blackie.

'Well, Martia, what do you think of that?'

'She sounds very English.'

'What do you mean?'

'Serious, stiff, you know, not someone you'd go raging with.'

'I'm not someone you'd go raging with either. I don't mind her being formal, after all she doesn't know me at all, and she does make a point of saying she's independent, and she twice asks me to not go to any trouble, I like that.'

'Now don't be a softie and spend hours ...'

'I'm not going to do that, but I do have some Forest and Bird booklets I can send her, and I can find a couple of web sites with intercity bus timetables. I don't know anything about cheap places to stay in Auckland though, 'cos I live here, I guess!'

'Apart from Chez-toi neither do I. Just watch yourself, Poppy, you're a real sucker for your Dad's protégées and they're not so good at doing anything for you. Anyway, I was wanting to ask if you'll come to a lesbian community meeting next week – on Wednesday at the Ponsonby Community Centre.'

'Community meeting? I didn't think there was a lesbian community any more, I thought we were all queers together these days.'

'Well, that's what the meeting is about, really. Some of the Lesbian Links group want to combine with the gay guys and whoever else "transcends heterosexuality" and form a single Queer Links phone line. I'm trying to get some of us old-fashioned lesbian feminists along, so at least we can make a point.'

'Martia! I'm surprised at you calling us old-fashioned. You of "feminism is not for posting" fame.'

'Yeah. Well, you would be discouraged too if you had this flyer in front of you. The words "women only", never mind "lesbian only" have become pejoratives apparently, and the only way to be is sisters and brothers together these days. Anyway, will you come to the meeting? Please? We could have a bite to eat together beforehand, no, after, the meeting's at six.'

'Okay, okay, I'm not going to make you grovel, even though you know very well how much I hate meetings like this. If it's at six I'll go from school and we can eat together afterwards and have a real catchup.'

As she put the phone down, Poppy was thinking about June 1977, the United Women's Convention, where she heard lesbians speaking out for themselves in public for the first time. Heterosexual women were asked to go home and say they were lesbian so they could experience the reactions of their family members; she and Kate had loved that.

Leaning against the wall, Poppy let the usual frozen stillness take over her body and waited to feel herself breathing again. Mrs Mudgely had jumped onto the telephone table and was purring against her arm.

'Nearly ten years,' Poppy heard. Mrs M was looking unusually solemn. 'Nearly ten years since she went. Almost as long as you were together.' Poppy shook herself back into life. 'Yes, I know, and I still miss her. More than I miss Rose, in fact. Maybe Rose was more right about some things than I was, maybe I did want Rose to be another Kate.' As she realised she was talking out loud to the cat, Poppy shook herself again. 'Time to blob out with the telly again, my cat friend. I'll reply to jane.blackie tomorrow night.

In the end, it was Sunday evening before Poppy got back to her computer. On Friday night after school she had gone to Stefan and May-Yun's for dinner. Their daughter Annie was there and Poppy had not seen her for several months; she had been in Sydney studying computer animation at the expense of the firm that employed her making television commercials. 'But not for much longer,' Annie told them over dinner. 'I'm going to make movies. Animated movies for adults. High quality. I've got some ideas about doing *Waiting for Godot* in one hundred per cent animation, it's so exciting! And I've got another idea, Mum, that would mean using the old photos of your family when they immigrated, I can scan them into the computer and create characters, and ... I want to talk to you about it while I'm here Mum, see what you think.' Poppy was enjoying her niece's enthusiasm, the excitement showing in her voice and her whole body.

Stefan said, 'And who is going to pay you to carry out all these bright ideas?'

'Oh Dad, you are so, so, …'

'Cautious,' interjected Poppy. 'Don't be a downer, Stefan, when has Annie not been responsible about money? I know you helped her get through university without a student loan, but other than that she's supported herself since she was seventeen.' She stopped as she saw Stefan reddening, with anger or resentment at her intervening she supposed.

May-Yun's quiet voice broke in, 'Annie, I would love to talk to you about doing a story about my grandparents. We would have to be very careful not to offend them, you know.'

'But they've been dead forever, you can't offend dead people.' Ivan's fourteen-year-old voice couldn't decide where it was pitched.

'You can offend the memory of a person. And I wouldn't be too sure about my grandmother not knowing what is going on myself.' May-Yun smiled at her younger son, then turned back to Annie. 'I have been thinking about how to keep alive my family's stories of coming to New Zealand from China, wondering if I should try and write them. If you made this animated film, would it be like a comic? Would it make their lives trivial?'

'Oh, no, Mum. I'll show you this story – it's in a book, but it will give you the idea – called *Maus*. It's a really moving story by a Jew about his father and the war, and it's all drawn like cartoons with the Jews as mice and the Nazis as cats, and it is so powerful and I reckon I could do something like it on film … Not with animals of course,' she added quickly, seeing the look on her mother's face. 'Although the way it is done in *Maus* is really cool and not at all disrespectful.' Annie watched as her mother's face relaxed, then leaned over and patted her father's arm. 'Don't grouch, Dad.'

'They say having children keeps you young. Well, you make me feel like an old fogey with your talk of doing serious stories in comics and animations. What's wrong with words in a book, may I ask?

Some of humanity's best thinkers have done wonderfully with words in a book. At least, young lady, I can be pleased that you know about Beckett. Thank goodness for an arts degree. I just hope Chan manages to make something of his, what is it, interior design course.'

At times like this Poppy envied her brother his family, and wished he was more appreciative of his children. They were all so connected to each other, even Chan, the middle child, who was intense and introverted and often felt his father's irritation. There was tension in the air now, but Annie was so sure, of herself and of her family's love, that she rode along on the tight air-waves, watching everyone, taking care but not deflating or diminishing herself. Looking around at them Poppy noticed that Ivan had reddened and was staring down at his plate. 'Maybe I am romanticising this family too,' she thought, 'but I do love them to bits, all of them.'

A few times over the years Poppy had been annoyed with both Stefan and May-Yun for the 'waste' of May-Yun's talents since their marriage. She and May-Yun had become close to each other in that terrible time nearly ten years ago and had both worked at staying friends. They had their best times together when Stefan was not around; May-Yun tended to defer to him in his presence. Poppy's attempts to talk to May-Yun about expanding her life had always been quietly and firmly deflected. 'I am a very fortunate woman, Poppy, I love my husband and my children and I am happy. Do not try to change me, as I do not try to change you.'

When Poppy was leaving she asked Ivan to walk with her to her car.

'Where's Chan tonight?' she asked him.

'Working.'

'What do you mean working? Studying, on a Friday night? Or at a job?'

'He asked me not to say.'

'Okay. I won't ask you to then. Would you tell him I'd love to see him, and to give me a ring.'

'Sure. You're pretty cool for an aunt. See ya Poppy.' And Ivan blushed again and ran back into the house.

Poppy's Saturday was taken up with preparation for school, shopping and baking for the pot-luck and housekeeping chores. 'You can scowl as much as you like Mrs Mudgely, the vacuuming will be done.'

'Hey, your famous banana cake.' Martia was stirring a bowl of pasta when Poppy put her plate on Mel's table. They hugged. 'Good to see you,' said Poppy, 'who else is here that we know?'

'A few, though there are plenty I've never met before. Some of them look so young. I guess Mel meets them at the bookshop, she seems to know everyone. Jan and Ruth are here, and I saw Rina … and here she is.'

'Poppy, kia ora, my friend.' Rina's hug squeezed the breath out of her. 'How's it going, girl? How's the teaching? Come and sit down and I'll tell you about my new job at the kohanga. It's a choice job, but I've sure had to learn to stand up for myself with the committee.' They moved out onto the deck overlooking the upper harbour, away from the noise of music and voices.

As the evening went on more women arrived, the pot-luck turned into a party and the left-over food became party snacks. At midnight Poppy was still there, and enjoying herself more than she had expected to. There had been one bad moment when Rose came in with someone Poppy didn't recognise, but she'd made herself go over and say 'hello' and ask after Rose's mother. 'Say hi to her from me.'

'Yeah, sure. How's things with you?'

'Fine. I had dinner at May-Yun and Stefan's last night. May-Yun was asking after you.'

'Tell her hi from me. I mean to call her, but, you know …'

'Yeah, I haven't called your mother, either.'

'It goes like that, eh? Good to see you Poppy,' and Rose was off to talk to someone on the other side of the room.

'Okay?' Dear old Martia.

'Yes. Thanks. I don't think I feel anything.'

'I'm glad to hear it. Come and get another wine.'

'No thanks, I'll have a juice, I'm driving home soon. Have you recruited anyone else for Wednesday's meeting?'

'I'm still trying. I appreciate you coming, you know.'

On Sunday morning Poppy slept late. She was still dozing, Mrs Mudgely in the crook of her legs, when there was a knock on the door. It was Chan, who had never come to her place on his own before. She asked him in, and got coffee brewing and croissants in the oven while he put chairs up out the back in the sun.

'Hey, this is good,' she grinned at Chan over her coffee cup, 'how'd you get here?'

'Buses. I changed at Newmarket, it was easy.'

'Well, this is great, being visited by my grown-up nephew. How's things?' She didn't want to sound like Katrina, but feared she did, then saw tears well up in Chan's eyes.

'Want to tell me about it?' He nodded. He was miserable, he told her. The Polytech course was a bore, interior decorating was stupid, his father disapproved of him, and he didn't know what to do with his life. He wanted to get a job and earn some money and go to China, the place in China where his great-grandparents had come from.

'What's stopping you from doing that?' This was harder than Poppy had ever imagined, she sounded condescending to herself, what about Chan?

'Dad will create if I don't finish my course and Mum will be upset … I don't know who I am, you know, I look more Chinese than Mum and people think I'm a new immigrant. And now Annie's got big ideas about doing a film and she and Mum are going over the old photos and they never even ask me if I'm interested.'

'Have you said you are?'

'Well, no. Annie is so, so I dunno, so enthusiastic, she takes things over and I can't find any room. I've got a job on Friday and Saturday nights at a café and Dad thinks I'm out partying. I'd save the money and just go without saying anything but I have to talk to Mum about names and places. When I was a kid I wouldn't listen when she talked about her family, I didn't want to know about it, I got teased for being "Chinese" and I didn't feel Chinese at all and I resented it, you know, I just wanted to be like all the other kids. Besides, if I talked to Mum I think she would say she had to tell Dad.'

'I think she would too. Why not talk to him yourself?'

'I don't want to talk to him. He'll go over and over stuff and lecture me. I just want to leave Poly and get a job and save the money and show him.'

'One day, when you were about four,' said Poppy, 'and Ivan was a tiny baby, you were squeezing his arm, harder and harder until he cried. Your mother said to you to be gentle with the baby and you said straight back, "I don't want to be gentle, I want to hurt him." I thought that was pretty spunky at the time. But you're not four now, you're more or less grown up, and I think it would be a very good idea if you talked to your parents, both of them, separately if that's easier. Will you?'

'You're sounding like a regular aunty now. Will you tell on me?'

'No. But I am encouraging you very strongly to tell them yourself. You might feel like punishing your father, but you don't have to actually do it, and punish yourself and your mother into the bargain.'

'I'll think about it. Hey, I've got another book for you.' Chan and Poppy both read science fantasy novels and swapped titles they found in second-hand bookshops. 'This one has a really cool courts system.'

After he left Poppy forced herself to update her pupil records register. It took longer than she expected but meant when it came to writing end-of-year reports she would be up to date.

The first email she spotted when she logged on was from Rose.
Hi doll.

 Great to see you at Mel's. Looking good. Coffee some time? Ring me
 R

Three irritations in a two-line email, that was pretty good going even for Rose. Poppy hated being called 'doll', and disliked Rose's truncated sentences ('Serves you right for being a school teacher. Just wait 'til you see text messaging, that'll really put you in a spin.') She had, and it did. The third irritation was Rose emailing to suggest coffee instead of just ringing and asking her. Poppy toyed with the idea of sending a message back that read, *You too. Yes. Suggest a time.* Instead she wrote,

Dear Jane Blackie,

I'm sorry I haven't answered your email sooner.

She deleted that and started again.

I am replying to your email regarding your trip to New Zealand. I have some web pages that might interest you, regarding tramping (you say 'hiking' we say 'tramping', same thing more or less). See below. The best sea-bird places are outside Auckland. I'm posting you some brochures I've got from earlier trips. There is a Forest and Bird website (see below also) and when you get here I can show you some places around Auckland on a map.

Regarding accommodation there are a lot of places but they tend to be fairly heavily booked, especially after school breaks up in December, and the America's Cup (that's a big yacht race) is filling up a lot of places according to the paper. There is more information on the Auckland Visitors' website. I hope this helps.

Regards,

Poppy Sinclair.

She read it through, frowned, and quickly added, *'You could stay in my spare room when you first get here if you like.'* Then she copied in the web addresses and sent it.

'There's no need for that stern look, Mrs M. George would be disappointed if I didn't offer. And it would be mean, I have got a truly spare room, you know. And if she really is fit she could walk to the museum from here. Or borrow my bike.' Then she told herself to stop and went to bed to start the book Chan had left her, called simply *Whorl*, which made her think of icecream, but she didn't have any left.

Next day there was a short, very polite and grateful reply, thanking her for the offer of a place to stay for the first few nights and saying she would get a shuttle, having already had instructions from George, from the airport and he had offered her his key, if she, Poppy was not likely to be home at about four p.m. the day she arrived. Poppy had forgotten George had a key. And it was still weeks away – this woman was hyper-organised. She discovered when she looked up the date in her diary, that November 7 was a Sunday, so emailed back that she would meet the flight. Flight number, airline, scheduled arrival time, time of departure from Brisbane came back by return.

Driving to the community centre after school and a session with the other teachers in her syndicate about the format for end-of-year reports, Poppy remembered how much she hated meetings where people were likely to disagree with each other. She supposed it went back to her childhood where nobody disagreed, not out loud anyway. While she understood that debate and argument were necessary to the development of ideas, she hated being there while it happened. 'What a wimp,' she said to herself. Even claiming the last carpark on the street didn't stop her from wishing she was almost anywhere else. Martia had saved her a seat in the hall. There were maybe twenty-five women sitting in a large circle, with chairs for a few more.

As she and Martia walked to Ponsonby Road an hour and a half later in search of a meal, Poppy said, 'Let's make this my treat. Please.'

'Okay. Thanks.' Martia put her arm through Poppy's. 'Though I'm the one that owes you really, for coming along. What you said was great.'

'I always feel so feeble and wishy-washy, but I'm damned if I'm going to have anyone tell me what I can call myself and I don't call myself queer and I won't be put down for sticking with "lesbian".'

'Well, your "statement from the heart" as the young queer dyke put it, got the meeting back on track when it was wandering off into theoretical abstraction. I mean, we were there to talk about the phone line, not to come up with a definitive definition of "queer".'

'Do you think the young women feel as patronised by us as we do by them?' asked Poppy.

'Probably. Can't be avoided, I guess. Different generations, different worlds and all that. Still, I am cheered up by the energy and passion of those young ones, and a Queer Line is better than no phone line at all.'

Poppy squeezed Martia's arm. 'You are my oldest, dearest friend, don't you ever forget that. I'm glad I came to the meeting and especially glad to be with you now.'

'Thanks, Poppy.' Martia squeezed back. 'I love you heaps, too. Hey, I found out that Mum can get a cleaner paid for and told her I would come and visit just as often as I do now but I wouldn't be doing any more cleaning. And she said that was nice, it would mean she had someone else to talk to! After me wearing myself out for months!'

They reached the local noodle house, looked at each other, both nodded and went in, waving to a couple they knew and settling at a table on their own.

4

1985

None of them was familiar with the western suburbs so it took ages to find the hall. It was dark too, and many of the street signs were oddly placed or obscured by trees. Eventually Kate spotted a side road crowded with cars and, sure enough, it was the one. There were three chartered buses in front of what turned out to be the hall, which was already three-quarters full when they went in.

At the strategy meeting earlier in the week they had agreed that they would arrive singly or in pairs but sit together as much as they could. Kate spotted one group near the front on the left, and headed for them. As they walked down the centre aisle, they saw another group still holding a few empty seats and waving to them but Kate strode on and Poppy followed. They took the last two seats near the front, completing a set of twelve lesbians, four in each of three rows. The people that surrounded them did not feel friendly.

Poppy's stomach was in a knot. She looked around. About a third of those in the hall were from Pacific Island countries as far as she could see, the rest were Pakeha, divided between the grey-haired – more women than men – and young teenagers, also more female than male.

Their group was turned in towards its centre, the women exchanging comments in low voices.

'There must be three hundred of them and thirty of us!'

'Did you see the buses? I'd heard they were bussing people to these meetings, just like they did to the women's forums.'

'I want to go home!' said someone, only half joking.

Alexa handed around slips of paper headed, 'Questions'. 'In case you can't think of one,' she whispered, 'if there is a question time we must get some of ours in.'

Poppy's question read, 'Why did you bring this Bill to Parliament,' and was clearly designed for Fran Wilde to answer.

The room gradually silenced as a man walked onto the stage. He eschewed the microphone, and stood at the front edge of the stage, still for a moment while he surveyed the room. The babble of voices gradually hushed. When he spoke Poppy jumped; his voice was both loud and mellow, his tone unctuous. He welcomed them all as 'children of god'.

'Speak for yourself,' muttered Kate.

His words poured over them, relentless waves of sound, praising god and damning the devil. Every time he said 'praise the lord,' amens and hallelujahs sounded around the hall.

Stunned, Poppy felt an urge to run, to get far away from the sonorous exhortations and the exalted responses. 'Fight or flight,' she thought, 'I guess this time it's fight.'

The event had been billed as a debate on the Homosexual Law Reform Bill that would, if passed, remove 'homosexual acts' from the Crimes Act and make discrimination against lesbians and gays illegal under human rights legislation. It was clear already that there would be no real debate at this meeting, that the event was set up for those wanting to express opposition to the Bill. Poppy felt very small, very out-numbered. She looked at Kate. Her partner was sitting so straight as to be almost rigid, right knee jiggling, eyes wide and bright, darting about.

'She's enjoying this!' thought Poppy. The man on the stage came to a halt as three more people walked out to join him. There was Fran

Wilde, the Labour MP who had put up the Private Member's Bill, and two men. It became clear that one was the main speaker, and one, the local mayor, would chair the proceedings.

The opponent of the Bill got up to speak first. He used anecdotes and quotes from the bible to paint a picture of homosexuals as immoral, predatory, particularly with regard to children, and worthless. Poppy looked around the group she was sitting in while he spoke. 'We are all decent, ordinary people,' she thought, 'not a demon among us, no better or worse than any other group of twelve people you might find in this city. And on the whole we don't hate anyone.' She felt absolutely miserable, as if there was no way she could show anyone here who was not 'like her' her human-ness, her ordinariness. The wall of prejudice was so pervasive, so strong, so mis-informed, so glued together with ignorance, there was no way she could see herself or anyone else penetrating it.

The applause for the first speaker was thunderous. When Fran Wilde stood up to speak there was complete silence until the two groups of women and some scattered women and men clapped. She spoke quietly, using the microphone, careful with her figures and information. Her reasoned points about equality, human rights and justice were such a contrast to what had come before that Poppy felt sure everyone present must be convinced by them, at the same time aware the silence was politeness, nothing more, and reasoned argument was not going to move this audience.

The question time that followed was chilling. People got up one after another, each with a diatribe of prejudice and hatred demonstrating mis-information and ignorance, creating an opportunity for their man to make a 'reply' that echoed and reinforced them. Once Averil, who was sitting two rows ahead of Poppy and Kate, managed to leap up as an elderly man sat down and direct a question to Fran Wilde, who strung out the answer, repeating much of her initial speech, as long as she could. Again there was the still, polite, absolutely closed quietness while she spoke.

When the man who had begun the proceedings stood, clearly for a final prayer, Poppy, Kate and their friends stood as one and filed quietly out, ignoring the glares of the three at the end of each row they had to squeeze past.

They huddled outside for a few moments, gradually joined by others, overwhelmed by the hatred they had felt surrounding them. 'God is love, huh!' muttered someone. As they drifted off, not wanting to be there when the hall emptied, someone wondered whether they should stay in support of Fran Wilde. 'There's some gay guys looking after her,' said someone else authoritatively enough for them all to walk away, grateful to escape.

When they got home to Grey Lynn, where even the street lights seemed accepting and the lights shining from house windows looked positively friendly, Kate poured herself a whisky, tossed it back and poured another, holding the bottle up towards Poppy, who said, 'No thanks.' Kate always offered and Poppy always said no.

'Don't look so miserable, honey,' Kate sat down beside Poppy and put an arm around her shoulders. 'There's not so many of them, or they wouldn't have to cart them from one meeting to another by bus and if we let them get us down, they win.'

'I suppose I've never actually been in a place where I could feel such animosity, and not only that, know that I was the target for it. I guess I've had a pretty sheltered life.'

'Well, yes, you have, but I thought you had heard Betty and Maude and Joan and all of them talking about the bars in the 'fifties and how they had to defend themselves from physical attacks all the time, from police as well as joe public.'

'Uh huh, I have. And I've read about it too, but I never related any of it to myself until tonight, it was always about other people. I never actually felt anyone hate me before.'

'My first time was when Mary's mother chased me out of her daughter's bedroom with a bread knife when I was in the fourth form. Though that might have been fear as much as hatred.

Whatever, I knew she didn't like me!' Then Kate grinned. 'Later I couldn't decide whether I was pissed off or pleased that she didn't know it was her daughter coming on to me.'

'Oh Kate, I remember you telling me about that, and I just thought it was, you know, a good story, because you got away. I never realised what you must have felt like. I'm sorry to be so naïve,' and Poppy tried to smile.

Kate took her by the shoulders and turned her so they were facing each other. 'Don't harden up, my sweet,' she said, looking into Poppy's eyes. 'One of the many wonderful things about you is your innocence. Don't let their bigotry get to you.' And she held her close, stroking her hair.

Poppy pushed her away. 'Innocence? I'm not a child, you know!'

'Okay, I know you're not a child, but you do see the best in everyone first. I guess what I mean is that you are not a hardened cynic like me, and I like that.'

'All right then.' Poppy was easily mollified.

After that night, there were stalls in Queen Street and the shopping malls, handing out pamphlets and talking to people who were mainly supportive, and, for Poppy, the anguish of the newspaper advertisement. Someone had the idea, to counter the anti-Bill petition that the Salvation Army and others were taking door to door, to show their supporters' numbers by having hundreds of people add their names to newspaper advertisements in all the main centres. The problem for Poppy was that there were two places she could put her name; in a section where people were identified as lesbians or gay men or in a section where signatories were identified only as supporters of the Bill.

Her concern was not her family, as it was for some, but her job as a teacher. Should she talk to her principal, about whose personal opinions she knew nothing? 'Nonsense,' said Kate, 'you don't need his permission, it's none of his business.'

'It's all right for her,' thought Poppy, then quickly felt ashamed of the thought. But it persisted. 'Everyone knows that heaps of nurses are lesbians. It's different for teachers, we are held much more responsible for children's opinions than we actually are; how could I deal with parents seeing me as a "bad influence", how could I do my job then?' It helped a little when she discovered that the names would be in random, not alphabetical order, and that support for the advertisements was so strong individual names would be very, very small.

In the end she added her name to the 'lesbians and gay men' list and nothing happened that she was aware of, so she felt a mixture of pleasure that she had taken the risk and regret that she had not taken it more boldly. A number of women and men around the country had their personal stories and photographs published; she admired every one of them enormously. Kate had talked about offering her story, but by the time she put herself forward there were enough. Poppy tried not to be relieved.

The great surprise to her was the whole-hearted way Katrina got involved with Heterosexuals Unafraid of Gays, commonly known by its acronym, HUG. 'It's disgraceful,' Katrina said on national television, 'to behave like playground bullies towards people who are different from you. Bigots should look to themselves, not others, when they talk of morality and being a bad influence on children; I certainly would not want any grandchildren of mine to be taught by people with such prejudice.'

'Oops,' said Kate, when the news clip had ended. 'Good support, not good strategy to talk about categories of people who should be teachers, good teachers is all they need to be. Like you,' and she took Poppy's hand. 'I don't think she likes me much, but she's a great mother, sticking up for her daughter like that. More than I could expect of mine.'

'Belinda's not used to being in public like Katrina,' said Poppy, 'don't be too hard on her. And I'm not at all sure Katrina is doing it for me, I think her sense of justice is outraged; perhaps she notices more because it's about me, but that's all.'

'Even better. Political belief and personal concern, that's the best combination of all. Come on, give her some credit.'

'I do, really.' But Poppy was unaccustomed to seeing her mother, who more often than not seemed to find her not quite up to scratch in some way or another, as her champion. Nonetheless, she was pleased and grateful that her family were standing up against what at times seemed like an incoming tide of prejudice and hatred that could swamp them all. Even Stefan, though she would never have known had not eight-year-old Annie told her about the man and woman who had come to the door with 'that petition they are talking about on the news,' and 'Daddy told them off a treat. I couldn't hear it all, but he said to "take that rubbish away from his house and find something better to do with your lives."'

Poppy still avoided meetings as often as she could; it suited her to have Kate go to them and then she would willingly take part in a stall or proof-read pamphlets, whatever tasks needed doing. Activity around the Bill continued all through the winter. Katrina asked to join Poppy and Kate for the Gay Rights march up Queen Street in September and turned up with May-Yun and Annie, so they all walked together. University Gays had made dozens of banners with the names and pictures of famous lesbians and gay men from the past, and Annie carried one with Eleanor Roosevelt on it all the way. Afterwards Katrina and Kate shared their outrage at the lack of media attention; Poppy played with Annie during the speeches and did her best to answer her questions about who Eleanor Roosevelt was.

The Bill became part of their lives, with every social encounter involving stories about the latest political moves or internal disagreements and how the anti-Bill petition was rigged, with 'signatures' from children, dead people or those who had left the country. Anecdotes about the way their friends responded when confronted at the door with a petition to sign abounded; tales of ripping it up, seeing which neighbors had signed and visiting them, flushing it down the toilet, or one person keeping the petitioners talking and another going around the neighbors ahead of them – these became common currency.

When the part of the Bill that took 'homosexual acts' by men out of the Crimes Act was passed in Parliament the following year Poppy was relieved to get back to ordinary life. So was Kate, except for occasionally missing the excitement.

5

1999

Poppy looked at the sign. JANE BLACKIE it said, in black felt pen on a piece of brown card. 'I'll feel like someone from Corporate Cars holding this,' she said to Mrs Mudgely. 'Maybe I'll recognise her from the photos George sent, and I'll bet he has shown her photos of me.' She couldn't find the photos but she did find some balloons left over from her last party at least five years ago. The first one burst as she blew it up, the second flew out of her hand as she tried to tie a knot in its neck and whizzed violently around the room. Mrs Mudgely vanished; balloons going bang was one thing, balloons flying frenetically around her was quite another. When she returned she circled the two inflated balls resting on the chair – her chair – and made herself comfortable on the sofa.

'Should I ring the airport and check the arrival time?' Mrs Mudgely didn't reply. 'Nah, I'll just go.' Scooping up *Whorl*, her keys and handbag, Poppy headed for the door, then turned back for the name card with its two balloons, one yellow, one blue, stapled to each top corner by their necks.

As she got into her car she noticed how messy it was, and hurriedly gathered up papers, food wrappers and general flotsam and stuffed it all into a supermarket bag that she found on the floor. The resulting bundle went into the milk section of the letterbox that hadn't seen a bottle in quite a few years. Driving to the airport was uneventful, the afternoon cloudy with patches of sunshine, and parking once she got there was comparatively easy for once. She found Jane Blackie's flight number on the screen – it was on time, due to land in ten minutes. Unusual, thought Poppy, to be coming via Brisbane on a trip from London. She read *Whorl* for fifteen minutes, until she noticed people coming through from customs and immigration, when she moved to stand where she could be seen, holding up her ballooned sign.

Twenty minutes later she was still standing in the same place, moving her weight from one foot to another, with one balloon remaining to decorate JANE BLACKIE. She had pulled the other off and handed it to a crying child in a pushchair, which earned her a grateful smile from the mother. Three times she had mis-identified women coming through the doors on their own and held her sign high, smiling in their direction, hoping no-one noticed her lower it again as they walked on past.

'Hello, I'm the Jane Blackie I think you are waiting for.' Shoving her handbag and book under her other arm, Poppy shook the proffered hand. Hazel eyes and hair to match; the colour of mangroves in the evening light.

'Are you, okay?'

'Yes, sure, sorry.' And she saw that the other woman had pulled out of her bag a smaller, unadorned, piece of card with POPPY SINCLAIR neatly written on it. Poppy smiled at her left shoulder.

'The balloon is a nice touch.'

'There were two, I gave one away to an upset child. I was surprised that you came in from Brisbane, most flights from London come via Singapore or LA. And it was on time too, that's pretty unusual as well.' Poppy realised she was babbling, so stopped, abruptly. Jane Blackie looked exhausted.

'Going the long way saved me three hundred pounds, but at this moment I am not sure it was worth it.' The English accent was unmistakable, though there was hardly a trace of the Yorkshire sound that had become familiar to Poppy on her trips to visit George.

'Don't stare.' Poppy blushed as she realised she nearly said it out loud. She busied herself with taking over the modestly loaded trolley and scrabbling in her bag for her keys.

'Look, if it's not all right for me to … if there's any problem, I can …'

'No, no, it's just fine. Come on, my car is quite close, you must be wiped out after that trip.' No make-up, comfortable-looking clothes, only one large piece of luggage; Poppy made herself notice these details, and found herself approving.

The half-hour drive to Mt Eden was easier for Poppy because she did not have to look at her passenger. 'You asked about coming from Brisbane,' Jane had said as they drove out of the airport carpark, 'I got a heavily discounted fare through a new kind of travel agent, a broker that works through the internet; they do only the minimum and guarantee you the cheapest fare. So I've come from London via Ankara and Singapore and Brisbane on two, no three, different airlines, and it's … um …' she consulted her watch, 'forty hours since I left Yorkshire. I have forgotten how many hours in the air and how many hours at airports. Please excuse me if I am not particularly coherent.'

'I'm the one who's not coherent,' thought Poppy, and said, 'That sounds ghastly. What about food, would you like a snack, or a meal, or is your body completely out of sync and you haven't a clue?'

' "Out of sync?" Oh, I see, the time difference. That, I think. What I would really like is a shower. I had one at the airport in Singapore but that seems a very long time ago.'

'A shower is easily arranged.' They drove along in silence, Jane looking about her. Mrs Mudgely was hovering just above the rear-vision mirror, looking sternly at Poppy. 'It's just a coincidence that she has the same eyes and hair as Kate. Kate has been gone nearly ten years. This woman knows nothing about her, it's nothing to do with her, get over it …'

'It was beautiful flying in to Auckland. So much water, and so green. Even the clouds were beautiful, light and puffy.'

'I guess we're kind of proud of it.'

'And the area we are driving through is very different from anything in Yorkshire. I have never seen so many houses built in wood. There is virtually no building in wood in Yorkshire. But you will know that, from visiting George. I think I remember him saying once that his daughter was staying. And he showed me photos before I left.'

'I've visited him and Susanna a few times, and you're right, about wooden houses here, not just in Auckland, but all around the country. And here we are, this is the wooden house that is chez moi.' Poppy pulled into the curb and gestured upwards, released the boot and jumped out to get the suitcase. 'No, no, let me take this up the steps, I'm used to them. Come and meet Mrs Mudgely.'

'Mrs …?'

'You'll see. In fact here she is, coming to meet us.'

'Oh', the laugh was relieved. 'Hello Mrs …?' She looked questioningly at Poppy, who managed to look back with only a slight intake of breath.

'Mrs Mudgely, and don't ask, I never explain her name.'

'Hello Mrs Mudgely'. Jane crouched down and stroked the cat between her ears. 'It is very nice to meet you.' She looked up and Poppy quickly looked away. 'I have a dog at home, a spaniel called Benjy. I miss him already.'

Once she had given Jane a tour of the house and left her to have a shower, Poppy gathered up Mrs Mudgely and retreated to her bedroom. 'What am I going to do?' she asked the cat, 'every time I look at her I see Kate.'

'It's a coincidence, get over it.' Mrs Mudgely looked unusually stern. 'She's a very nice person, very well-mannered in fact, look after her like a proper host and forget the past.'

'Oh Mrs Mudgely, you've been won over by a bit of attention and flattery. Just like that! And you're right, of course, I do have to get over her having the same colouring as Kate. Everything else about her is different from Kate, the way she moves, her skin, how she talks, everything.'

6

1990

Kate was getting ready for a seven o'clock start at the hospital, and Poppy lay in bed, drowsy and happy from their love-making. School didn't go back from the summer holidays for another three weeks, so she could wallow in the warmth and smells of the bed for as long as she wanted. When Kate came in naked from the shower she opened her eyes enough to enjoy the sight of her lover rummaging in her clothes, on a chair and in the wardrobe.

'Come here, gorgeous.'

Kate grinned at her, 'No way. I'm late enough already. I'll pick up a carton of white and a bottle of whisky on my way home; we're nearly out of both.'

'Golly, they've gone fast, must be the social season.'

She flung her arm around Kate's neck when she came, dressed, to kiss her goodbye. 'Shan't let you go.'

'Temptress! Ward sisters have to set a good example, you know; you were the one who was so keen that I should better myself.'

'Mmmmmm,' she nuzzled into Kate's neck. 'Be properly rewarded for what you do, more like. Okay then, go. Off with you! And don't forget your sword and armour.'

'I may just need them, Consultant Ken, scourge of the nurse's station is back today.' Kate kissed her again, peeled her arm away and was gone.

Poppy blew a kiss as Kate dashed out the door, and listened for the sound of her car starting and pulling out into the street. Hugging her pillow, she revelled in the engulfing happiness and the wonder that she, Poppy Sinclair, the outsider, the detached one, should love and be loved so thoroughly, so beautifully, so perfectly. Her worries last year had been groundless. Kate's preoccupations with work had been just that, dealing with hospital politics and a ghastly patient death. Once Kate's holidays had started and they had got away to Hahei everything had come right again.

It hadn't begun well. Katrina had dropped by in the morning, to 'wish you Happy New Year, my dears, seeing we didn't see you at Christmas, before you go away in your tent.' Kate had giggled and said, 'We're not actually leaving in the tent, Katrina, just sleeping in it when we get there.'

'Yes, yes dear. Now look,' she turned to Poppy, 'John and I are going to Noumea on the 4th, for about ten days. Would you be a sweet pea and pop in once to water the house plants? You know how to do the security, don't you, and here's the key.'

'I'm not sure when we'll be back,' said Poppy, 'it might be better if you asked Stefan.'

'Oh dear, I haven't got time to go out there. John's got some people coming for lunch and so many social engagements arranged before we go, please be a dear and drop the key out to him on your way out of town.'

'It's hardly on our way,' Kate said and got a sharp glance from Katrina before she turned, smiling, back to Poppy.

When she had gone, Kate said, 'Well, sweet pea, what other messages shall we do for your family on the way?'

'Oh Kate, don't be cross, she hardly ever asks me to do anything, and it's not far out of our way.' Then the traffic had been really heavy all the way across town to Pakuranga and they had had a coffee with

Stefan and May-Yun and Poppy got involved in a game of snakes and ladders with Chan that took them both up the ladders and down the snakes relentlessly for a full twenty minutes. 'I used to be able to cheat and let him win,' Poppy said in an apologetic aside, 'but not any more.'

When they finally got back to the southern motorway it was choked and they crawled all the way to the Coromandel turnoff. Kate had pulled in to the pub at Pokeno.

'Come on girl, five o'clock and we're on holiday and it's a fine, sunny day.'

It was Poppy's turn to drive, so she had a low alcohol lager. Kate ordered a whisky and a beer. She held the whisky glass up to Poppy. 'To holidays. It's so good to get away from that hospital. No shifts, no doctors, just you and me and the sun and the sea. What a shame we can't take *Swift*.' She laughed at the look on Poppy's face at the thought of taking Kate's latest sail boat on holiday with them. 'Okay sweet, just joking.'

Poppy smiled at her. 'Oops. Sorry to be so obvious. Just think of it though, no preparation, no children, no families, no friends, just you and me. This is what I like best of all, Kate, when you and I go off camping together. This time we have a whole eight days.'

They both really relaxed into the holiday once they had the tent up and the campsite organised to Poppy's satisfaction.

New Year's Eve had been perfect; fresh smoked fish, French bread and wine on the beach, swimming naked in the dark, making love in the tent to the explosions of camping ground's family fireworks display ('Reminds me of your fruit machine the first time I kissed you') and holding each other and kissing through the horns and drunken cheers at midnight.

Lying in their bed with the memories, the sound of Kate's car fading, Poppy abandoned the pillow and hugged herself, holding in the happiness, her eyes filling with tears.

Suddenly it was nine o'clock and Poppy woke with a start, hot and sweaty. She had fallen asleep and she was meeting Katrina at ten for coffee. Standing in the shower, as hot as she could bear it, needles of water pricking at her scalp and her back, Poppy sang herself a medley of Dusty Springfield songs.

When she arrived at the café on Ponsonby Road at exactly ten there was no sign of Katrina so she sat down at a table just inside the windows that opened on to the footpath. As soon as she had taken out her diary and started making a list of things to do before school started, Katrina appeared in the doorway.

Her mother kissed at her cheek and sat down. 'I'm sorry to be late, dear, a last minute phone call. Are there waiters here or do we go to the counter?'

'I'll go, what will you have?'

When they were settled with coffees and a large piece of carrot cake for Poppy – 'Breakfast', she said to her mother's disapproving look – Katrina said, 'Well, this is nice, mother and daughter having a tete-a-tete. How are you, dear.'

'I'm absolutely wonderful,' said Poppy. 'Kate and I are so happy.'

'That's lovely, Poppy. I did worry for a while, when you first told me about liking women, whether you would be happy.' Katrina sat back in her chair and appraised her daughter. 'You look it, too.'

'I am Mu – Katrina, I am, so happy. It will be thirteen years this year that Kate and I have been together. That's longer than you've managed since you divorced George. We're talking about buying a house together, or a weekend place by the sea, where Kate can keep her bo – yacht, it's a yacht.'

'That's nice.' Katrina leant over the table and squeezed Poppy's hand, 'I am so pleased for you dear, and Kate, of course.'

'It's okay, I know Kate has never been a big hit with you but I can't understand why you don't like her more.'

'I'm sorry if you've noticed, dear. It's her parents really, Bob and Belinda Smith, I don't like. He's so smarmy and she, well, she made an utter disgrace of herself at the Heart Foundation dinner last year, I think she was drunk before she arrived. I was so relieved we weren't at the same table.'

'Please don't. Kate is not her parents. She's, well, she's Kate and I love her very much.'

'Yes, I'm sure you do. You're like your father in that way.'

'What do you mean?'

'Loving. Putting everything into a relationship, caring so much about the other person, so certain that loving them is enough.'

'Whatever are you on about?'

'I'm sorry, dear. I'm really talking about me and George, not you and Kate, you two are quite lovely together.'

'That's a patronising thing to say. But what do you mean about you and George?'

'Well, I'm not sure one should talk to one's children about these things. I'm sorry I raised it. Oh, I suppose you are grown-up now, you might as well know, not that there's anything much to know. George and I were very much in love at first and then, well, he has no real ambition, he wanted to have time for the family he said, not be at work all hours and he was so involved with his blessed insects. You know, I think I've managed to forget what they're called … tri … something flies. Oh, how I came to hate the silly little creatures!'

'Trichoptera. Caddis flies.'

'Oh, yes. Well, I'm sorry dear, but your father got very boring over the years, he never wanted anything to be any different, never wanted to extend himself, just to plod on in the same old way, and I like being busy, being part of the big wide world, moving and shaking in small ways, making decent money, you know …'

'Yes, I know.' Poppy couldn't remember her mother ever saying as much about herself and George before, she was feeling quite emotional at it, and more affection for her mother than she had in a long time.

'Then you and Stefan were off in your lives and George and I were living more or less separately from the same house and he fell in love with Susanna.' Katrina laughed. 'I was so startled. I thought it would be me that went off with someone else, I thought he would never actually do anything about anything. He came to me and said he had fallen in love and wanted a divorce. I was stunned, relieved, scared and excited all at once.

'Once I saw him and Susanna together I could see they were absolutely suited to each other so I gave them my blessing. We both felt guilty about you, though, you seemed to have this idea that we were going to be old fogeys together forever. Stefan said he saw it coming, but you made us both feel very guilty. How old were you?' Katrina answered her own question. 'Eighteen and at Teachers' College, and you made George and I feel like we were committing a terrible crime giving up on a bad job of a marriage.'

Poppy was embarrassed. 'I didn't realise I made it harder for you. And I was really shattered. I had this picture of us as a happy family. Stefan told me once I was a Pollyanna about it.'

'Never mind, dear, it's all in the past now. And I am glad you are happy.'

'Are you happy?'

'Yes, of course. I have a good job I like and a nice place to live – two good things came out of my second marriage, the name Lancaster and my place in Herne Bay – and John and I suit each other very well.'

'What's wrong with Sinclair?' Poppy was suddenly defensive of her and her father's and brother's name.

'Nothing for your generation, probably. But you see I'm the same generation as "the" Sinclairs, you know all those famous brothers. I got sick and tired of people asking me if I was related to Keith, or Geoff, or … I forget the others' names.'

'Oh. I see, I suppose. Why have you never married John? You could have married him and kept the name Lancaster you know.'

'No, that's not why we've never married. Pomare is a fine name, but he is very involved with his iwi land claim and his family were worried about inheritance problems if we got married, and I thought two weddings were quite enough for one woman, and so we never have.

'I don't have a lot to do with his family, nor he with mine as you know, and that suits us both. He has his iwi responsibilities and he takes them very seriously but he doesn't want to live in Northland, not yet anyway. We have a good life together here in town and I don't mind being on my own when he's away. He's going to be particularly involved with iwi matters this year, with it being the one hundred and fiftieth anniversary of the Treaty, but I've got a busy year coming up too. I suppose things may get more difficult when he retires, but we'll cross that bridge when we come to it. Heavens dear, you have got me talking on this morning.'

'I know. I like it. I wish we talked about real things more often.'

'Poppy dear, you and I just have different ideas about what "real" is.'

'While I've got you to myself …' As she spoke Poppy realised that she and her mother were hardly ever together on their own, there was always Kate, or Stefan and his family, or John, even occasionally, all of them at once, but she couldn't remember when she and Katrina had last been together, just the two of them.

'While I've got you to myself, why don't you have anything to do with your – our – Greek relations.'

'Oh my goodness.' Katrina looked at her watch. 'You know all that history, I'm sure you've heard it all before.'

'Yes, but only in bits here and there. And I'm wondering whether John's close ties with his whanau and all that make you want to, you know, explore your own roots or something.'

Katrina laughed. 'Oh no, dear, not me. I'm one for looking forward, not back.'

'Well, tell me about your parents again, anyway.'

'You're a funny, sentimental thing, like your …'

'Father. I know. Tell me.'

'Well, I was born in 1930, so my parents must have come here in about 1928 from Melbourne when they were in their late thirties. This is silly, I feel like I am giving a lecture.'

'Don't worry about that, just tell me.'

'Well, they were both born in Melbourne, surely you remember that, and neither of them ever went to Greece; their parents were early Greek immigrants into Australia. And, I know I never told you this bit before, I think they came to New Zealand because of the shame of not having had children. It's hard to believe it now, but they had been married six or seven years when I was born, and a couple of things my mother said over the years made me think that not having had children was something of a disgrace. Once I thought my mother might have had an abortion when they were first married, there was one little comment she made a year or two before Poppa died, so maybe they thought it was their fault there were no children in the marriage. It wasn't something I ever asked either of them about.

'Anyway, whatever the reason, they had been married for seven years and they had no children when they came here, and Poppa got work in the railway workshops. I think I was a real surprise! Then the depression came, and Poppa kept his job but only just and he had no pay rises for something like seven years, and we were poor but not as badly off as some. Your Nana would give away food, to children that came to the door. I remember that, I was scared of those children. We lived in this awful house in the gully in Parnell until the end of the war.' Katrina shuddered at the memory of it. 'Poppa was too old to go to war, so he wasn't allowed to leave his job, he had to stay and "keep the trains running" as Nana would say.

' "Don't look back, always look forward", Poppa would say to me. He was proud of me, "his clever girl". He was always so active I didn't expect that he would die first. Do you remember him at all?' Katrina got a tissue from her handbag and carefully wiped under her eye make-up. Poppy nodded.

'A little bit. I remember a stooped old man who patted my head and took me on walks to the dairy to buy us both icecreams. Oh, and he taught me cribbage, and cheated in the scoring – I don't think he liked me beating him.'

'That would be right, I think I got a certain competitiveness from him.' Poppy was silent. 'All right, don't flatter your mother, then. Nana lived another five years, but I don't know how much she knew about the last three or four of them. She faded into herself after Poppa died and didn't eat unless someone put food in front of her. George and I talked about having her to live with us, he would have, it was me who couldn't do it and there was nothing left when she died, it all went on the nursing home. I couldn't be sorry in the end, she was just a shell. You know, I can hardly remember what she was like before that.

'Heavens, look at the time! I'm due to meet John at the cardiologists in fifteen minutes.'

Poppy started and her musings about her mother's family vanished like a bubble touching the ground. 'Cardiologist! What's wrong?'

'Not me dear, John. He's been having some chest pain. Nothing to worry about his doctor said, but I insisted on a cardiologist, I don't want him dying on me, and neither does his family, he's the one driving their claim at the Tribunal. Lovely, lovely to see you dear, we must do this again.' And she was gone.

Poppy sat and waited for the flurried air to settle around her, wondering whether she would ever feel that her mother treated her as an adult and about how often she had been called 'dear'. Shaking off her irritation at being patronised and holding on to the warmth she felt at her mother's self exposure, she resolved to arrange more of these meetings, to ask more questions, to get to know Katrina better, to convince her that she, Poppy, was a fully functioning adult. Somewhere she had read that parents did not perceive their daughters as adults until they had married and had children of their own. She sighed heavily at the thought.

The young man behind the coffee machine was looking at her. Oh heavens, had her sigh been that obvious? She waved and smiled at him and set off down Ponsonby Road towards school, enjoying the life in the street, waving at an occasional acquaintance and grateful that after all those years of driving to Mangere she now had a job at a school she could walk to. She'd spend a couple of hours beginning to get her classroom ready for this year's class and be home when Kate came in after her shift. A picnic at Pt Chev beach would be nice; she'd make a quiche when she got in, an asparagus quiche, she decided, spotting some in the fruit shop display that spilled over onto the footpath.

It was after four when Poppy walked the five blocks home from school. She had become involved in planning the layout of her classroom for the coming year and the time had flown past. Kate's car wasn't out the front, so she wasn't home yet. When Poppy got inside and saw the wine cask and whisky bottle on the bench she was perplexed, until she saw the note. *Shitty shift, beautiful day, I've gone sailing. Back by seven. Love you K.*

Poppy tried not to feel disappointed. There had been few opportunities for Kate to sail lately and she did love it so. Occasionally, on a very fine day with not too much wind, Poppy would go, though she never enjoyed it and usually felt that she had dampened Kate's pleasure. A few times they had driven over to Bayswater together and she had spent the time at the house with Belinda, but they didn't have much to talk about and Belinda's attempts to refill her glass without Poppy noticing were somehow demeaning of them both. The last time Belinda had started talking about her husband and his affairs and what she had to 'put up with' and got tearful talking about what a wonderful child Kate had been and how badly she wanted grandchildren, all the while denigrating herself and how little she had done with her life. Poppy found it unbearable and went for a walk then sat by the jetty and watched Kate sail in.

'Don't you worry about her?' she had asked on the way home.

'Who, Mum? Not much. As long as Dad doesn't actually leave her, she'll be all right.'

Poppy roused herself and set about making the quiche, thinking about the day. Did Kate share her mother's view that she was sentimental? That was her key in the door, and it was only six. Poppy quickly slid the quiche into the oven, set the timer, and went out to greet her. Kate was in the living room pouring herself a whisky.

'Hello, pet. Drink?' Poppy shook her head and stood admiring Kate's shining eyes and hair.

'Good sail?'

'Wonderful, just wonderful, quite a wind out there.' Kate shook her head and laughed. 'Exhilarating, I nearly went over once. Don't be a silly worry-wart,' she added at the look on Poppy's face, 'you know I can manage her, and a dunking in the harbour is no risk at this time of year, the water's as warm as a bath.'

Poppy supposed that feeling patronised was a hangover from the morning's session with her mother. She hugged Kate and kissed her on the mouth. 'I'm glad you enjoyed it, your note said work was shitty.'

Kate swallowed her drink and poured another. 'Oh, Poppy, I don't know whether I am cut out to be a staff nurse, or even a nurse any more. I shouted at Creepy Ken today, when he was dispensing leers and his own hands in the nurses' station and he complained to matron. She was okay, but she also told me there are more cuts coming, and the whole atmosphere is awful, just awful. I think I need a new job.'

'You're a good nurse Kate, the best. It will be all right.' Poppy drew her over to the couch and sat beside her with an arm around her.

'I guess. And what else could I do?' She dropped her head onto Poppy's shoulder, picked up her hand and stroked it. 'I love you Poppy. You are so dependable and reliable …'

'… And fierce and sexy …' interrupted Poppy, jumping down and crouching on the floor making lion noises that turned into a licking motion.

Kate smiled, rumpled her mane and patted the seat beside her. 'It's comfort I need just now, love. As well as everything else Mum was more boozed than usual this afternoon and wanted to tell me about Dad's new secretary – she said it in quotes – and started crying and hanging onto me and calling me her girl. I know I should be more sympathetic but it sickens me.'

'Poor you. And poor Belinda. I had coffee with Katrina this morning and we had the most amazing conversation. Do you want to hear about it?'

Kate nodded, and they sat talking, arms around each others' shoulders, until the oven timer went off.

'The quiche?' Poppy jumped up. 'Picnic at the beach or at home?'

'At home,' and Kate got up to set up the outside table.

The first term of the new school year started, as usual, at the end of January, in the hottest part of the summer. By the end of the first week Poppy knew the names of all the children and who were going to be her greatest challenges for the year. By the end of the second week she had routines established with all but the two most recalcitrant children, one of whom was, unusually, a girl. She resolved to find out more about the two and see if she could bring them on board with the rest of the class before Easter.

February 14th, Valentine's Day, was on the Wednesday of the third week of term. Poppy and Kate always bought each other a silly card, and this year was no different. They exchanged them in bed and had a long cuddle. When Kate had a day shift and started at seven Poppy got up early with her on weekdays; if she got to school at seven or soon after she had a wonderful hour on her own in her classroom, doing planning or marking when she was not tired after a day's teaching. As they were getting dressed, Kate said, 'If the wind doesn't drop away completely I think I'll go out for a sail this afternoon, the tide's marginal for getting back in but if I go straight from work I should be out and back before the tide is too far out. How about we go out for a Valentine's dinner afterwards? Somewhere nice, I'll ring and make a booking in my break. My treat.'

Poppy nodded vigorously. 'Yes, yes, I'd love to go out to dinner,' she said.

7

1999

A green salad, chicken, sliced ham, a couple of Kapiti cheeses, some crusty bread and a bowl of fresh strawberries for dessert. Poppy thought that should make a meal or a snack, whatever Jane fancied. And after tonight, she resolved, she wouldn't be doing meals or any other looking after. She set out the food on the dining table and some chairs at the picnic table outside then went and knocked at Jane's door.

'Would you like something to eat?' she called out.

Jane appeared, wearing a white cotton shirt and white trousers, her hair still wet from the shower.

'Cricket?' asked Poppy, moving her hands into position on an imaginary bat.

Jane looked confused. 'Cricket? I haven't played for years.'

'Sorry,' said Poppy, 'Bad joke. English person, white clothes …'

'Oh,' Jane laughed uncertainly. 'Did you mention food? I am hungry now, I could make some scrambled eggs or a have a piece of toast …'

'Sorry,' repeated Poppy, 'for teasing that is. And I've got some food ready, I thought we could take it outside.' Gesturing towards the table, she saw Mrs Mudgely watching from the doorway, one paw raised, her look questioning. 'That's quite enough from you.'

'I beg your pardon?' said Jane. Poppy felt her self blush. She had spoken out loud. This was awful, awkward and embarrassing, she didn't seem to be able to say anything sensible.

'Sorry.' For heaven's sakes, how often was she going to say 'sorry'? 'Help yourself to some food, I'll get us a drink. Water? Beer? Wine?'

'A glass of water would be very good, thank you.'

By the time they were both sitting under the magnolia tree, Poppy had gathered herself together. 'I'm really quite sensible,' she said, looking at the tree behind Jane, 'you have to be to teach nine-year-olds. I've just not had too many strangers to stay in my house lately, and, well, sometimes I talk to my cat.' She stopped. This was no better.

'Would you rather I went somewhere else. I could arrange something tomorrow, I am sure. The people at the museum offered to help.'

'No. No, please don't.' Poppy's voice was more definite than she had expected. 'I'd like you to stay, really. I'm sorry I'm being such a klutz.' She did her best to direct a friendly smile at the other woman, feeling Mrs Mudgely's softness on her leg. As the silence lengthened she leant down to stroke the cat, stopping herself from gabbling on, avoiding looking anywhere near her guest. She took a deep breath, and looked up at Jane, 'Look, I'd better explain ...' she began, at the same time as Jane said, 'The museum people really did offer ...' and they both stopped and looked at each other.

Poppy sat up straight and held up a hand so she could speak first. 'I'm sorry I keep saying sorry.' She smiled. 'And that I have been behaving a bit oddly. It's just that your eyes and hair are the same colour as, well, someone who was very important – a long time ago – and I've been a bit thrown by that.'

She made herself look at Jane and felt the tension slip away a little. Her eye and hair colouring was the same as Kate's, but otherwise she was quite different. Kate's face had been wider and livelier, her skin more olive, and tanned, her expression always changing, her head and hands constantly moving, making gestures, pushing her hair back, looking around her, while Jane had a pale complexion and was comparatively still, her expression careful, considering, her body quiet, with small, slow movements.

'Oh, I see. Thank you for telling me. I was beginning to wonder whether you really could not abide house guests and were being polite for your father's sake.' Jane's smile really did light up her face, thought Poppy.

'Oh no, nothing like that. I've been trying not to look at you is all, so I wouldn't gabble, and that made it worse. It's okay now that I have said it and, really, you don't look that much like Kate.' Poppy hesitated, then went on. 'Please, don't rush off, I would feel really bad if I had driven you away, and you can see I really do have the space for you to stay.'

'Thank you, I like it here already, the room is delightful and the view up the hill is grand, and your garden – and, if I am reading my map correctly, it is not too far to walk to the museum. However, you did offer me only the first few days and the people at the museum have said they will find me somewhere to settle for the rest of my time in Auckland. I will find out more tomorrow and perhaps we can talk about it again then. And thank you for preparing this wonderful food, it is so ... so ... Mediterranean, and that makes me think I am on holiday. Which I am not, of course, but it is a very nice feeling,' and she smiled again. Mrs Mudgely had moved to a patch of grass between them and was washing herself with every appearance of indifference.

As the two women ate and talked they both relaxed a little. Poppy learned that Jane's first degree was in ornithology and her special interest was common sea-birds such as cormorants and gulls and terns. She hadn't completed her MA thesis, in spite of spending four months in Scotland studying sea-bird nesting colonies, because her mother had become ill and she had returned to Whitby, on the

Yorkshire coast where she grew up, to be near her parents and somehow the degree had never been finished. After a few years working in the local museum she had begun a masters again, this time in Museum Studies at Leicester University, supporting herself with a part-time job at the museum there. Because her mother's health was bad she took the long train journey home many weekends. In 1985, with a Masters in Museum Studies (Zoology), she started full-time work as a keeper, then a curator, at the Cleveland Natural History Museum in Middlesbrough, a nearby town much bigger than Whitby. 'I still prefer live birds to stuffed ones and, of course, I am responsible for more than the birds, my title is Natural History and Exhibitions Curator, but I somehow just stayed on.'

'My father died in 1986, suddenly, of a heart attack, so I had to stay near my mother, who had chronic emphysema, and when she died about seven years ago, I thought of looking for a position in Manchester or London, but somehow I never got around to it.'

As Poppy talked about her teaching, the mosquitoes began their evening attack, so they moved inside for coffee. 'I am not a true Englishwoman, I do not like tea,' Jane had said. Soon after it was dark she went to bed. 'The travelling has caught up with me, I can hardly keep my eyes open.' Poppy explained that she would be leaving for school soon after seven and would leave a key on the table if Jane wasn't up.

'Birds, museums and parents, nothing about marriage or relationships, did you notice that, Mrs M?' They were in bed, too. Poppy made a desultory effort to read more of *Whorl*, but was finding the book's focus on the social systems of its twenty-second century world rather than people's lives, was not holding her attention.

'No siblings, not that she mentioned anyway, a bit formal in her ways. Organised though, I reckon she will look after herself. What say we ask her to stay on?' Mrs Mudgely's purring faded as cat sleep settled on her.

At a quarter to six next morning Poppy was wide awake. Usually she stirred reluctantly at the alarm forty minutes later. 'Serves me right for going to bed so early,' she grumbled, and got up. Jane was sitting at the dining table, with a cup of coffee, the duvet off her bed around her shoulders. There was a map of Auckland spread out on the table. 'Good morning. I hope I did not disturb you. I woke at four, I think my body clock is still in Singapore or somewhere.'

'No, you didn't disturb me, I've just woken up,' Poppy waved a hand towards the bathroom. 'I'm heading for the shower. Did you find everything you wanted? Apart from the heater, that is.'

'Yes, thank you, and I have not needed a heater, honestly. Can I make you a coffee while you are in the shower? And some toast, perhaps. Or I do very good scrambled eggs.'

'Just coffee, thanks, it's too early to eat for me.'

While she showered Poppy tried to figure out whether her urge to invite Jane to stay for as long as she was in Auckland was a silly idea influenced too much by an opportunity to please George or a sensible inclination to have some friendly company, or came from a tortuous emotional need to be reminded of Kate, or … 'Stop it,' she told herself, stepping out of the water and towelling her hair more vigorously than necessary. 'Just let it happen or not. And you mind your business,' as Mrs Mudgely came in for a drink from the shower floor. She walked into a dining room smelling of coffee. Jane was eating toast. 'This raspberry jam is wonderful. Are you sure you will not have some?' She held up the half-eaten slice without noticing that jam dripped onto the floor, though Mrs Mudgely did.

'Yes, okay, you've changed my mind. I'll get dressed. And that coffee smells good.' Mrs Mudgely was purring around Jane's ankles and did not follow Poppy into her room. Poppy told herself she didn't mind at all; the cat was probably waiting for more jam.

She was unaccustomed to finding her clothes uncoordinated and shabby as she did this morning, pushing items back and forth in the wardrobe for several minutes before settling on grey cotton trousers and a red shirt. When she returned to the diningroom Jane poured coffee and passed a plate with two pieces of toast across the table. She had pen, paper, phone book and map spread around her.

'Is this a good time to talk about arrangements?' she asked.

'Yeah, sure.'

'I go to the museum this morning. Peter Voss, my contact there, said he would pick me up at nine. I think I might not last the day. How long does it take to adjust to the change in time zones?'

Poppy shrugged. 'It varies, a lot. One to four days, I guess.'

'Oh, heavens. I suppose no one will be surprised if I am a bit flummoxed then. I thought I would spend the morning at the museum and walk back and maybe walk down to the shop, the one there.' She pointed at the location on the map of the closest supermarket. The yellow pages was open at 'supermarkets and grocers'. 'And if you are in this evening, we could perhaps talk about how long I will stay; I will know a lot more then about, well, everything. I am a little embarrassed that I have arrived with so few arrangements made, and that you might feel obliged to have me stay here for longer than suits you.'

'Whoa!' Poppy did not know that she was genuinely smiling at Jane for the first time. 'I've got to leave for school in a couple of minutes, the traffic is all over the place on Harbour Bridge now that the America's Cup has started. How about you take my word for it that I am not feeling put upon, and I think I would like to have you stay and we talk about what happens from here on again tonight. I'll be home from school about five, and I could drive us both to the shops then. Oh, keys.' She scrabbled in the bowl on the sideboard and produced a New Orleans key ring with two keys on it. 'Back door, lock it from the inside and pull the bolt. Front door, that locks when you close it behind you, and this one will let you in. Please check that all the windows are closed when you leave – there's a bit of a problem around here with daytime burglars. Heavens, if I don't go right now, it will take me half an hour to get onto the motorway. See you later.'

'Tarra,' said Jane and put her elbows on the table, her hands wrapped around the coffee mug, sipping at it now and then. She knew her feelings of dislocation were due to more than jetlag and being in a place that was so much more different from England than she had expected. She and Héloise had had the biggest argument of their eight and a half years the night before she left. It had started as yet another discussion about Héloise wanting to have a child. 'It would be our child,' she had said. Jane had tried to speak quietly and reasonably, unaware that her hands were at her throat.

'I do not want to have a child, truly. We have been over this before, and I am sorry, but I cannot pretend; this is too important to pretend …'

'You mean you have been pretending about other things? What? Tell me?'

'No, that is not what I meant.' As she spoke Jane had wondered whether she was being entirely truthful. Had she been pretending to share Héloise's preoccupation with the house and garden in the past few years? Did she really want to be settled in this comfortable domesticity for the rest of her life? She didn't know, she just didn't know, but she did know that the idea of taking on twenty years of responsibility for a child made her feel suffocated, strangled, like she couldn't breathe. Héloise did not seem able to see that she was not being 'difficult' or waiting to be persuaded, she really, seriously did not want to be involved in bringing up a child.

'Oh heavens,' Jane thought, bringing herself back to the dining-room in the house in Mt Eden, Auckland. 'I have not even rung to say I have arrived. What is the time now in England?'

There were a total of twenty-three numbers to put in to use her phone card to call home; finally she heard the phone ringing and imagined the hallway in her – their –house. Jane was wondering if Benjy had barked once when the phone started ringing as he usually did, and was then ashamed of the relief she felt when she heard her own voice on the answer-phone. The message she left was short, too short, she thought, her hand still on the receiver; should she ring again? No, she should be able to email from the museum. There was just time before Peter Voss was due to get her papers ready and herself prepared for the meeting with the museum staff later this morning.

Peter Voss was on time, and took her on a tour of the museum introducing her to people. The meeting was casual but businesslike, the people friendly and interested in her project; by the end of the morning she was feeling overwhelmed by offers of hospitality that included weekends in the country, scenic tours of Auckland and baches at the beach. She had to ask about 'bach at the beach', which sounded to her like 'beach at the beach' at first. Peter Voss had been most pressing with his invitation for her to stay at his home in Birkenhead, with himself and his wife and his two teenage boys. Jane was genuinely grateful for all the offers she received and did not commit herself to any of them, pleading a brain too jetlagged to make arrangements and, in fact, by midday her eyelids were heavy, she had dropped all her papers on the floor twice and was ready to accept a ride back to Mt Eden.

She was falling asleep on her bed in Poppy's spare room, Mrs Mudgely purring in the crook of her knees, watching the cows on the side of the hill – she would have to learn to say 'Maungawhau' – when she remembered she had done nothing about emailing Héloise. After a nap, she decided, she would walk to the local shops and look for an internet café. She supposed that Mrs Mudgely changing position was not to remind her that there was a perfectly good computer with email access here, and Poppy was bound to be as generous about that as she was about everything else – when she wasn't looking at her like a frightened rabbit in car headlights.

Her reluctance to talk to Poppy about Héloise was no greater than her reluctance to talk to anyone else, she told herself; this was time out from all that, time to clear her own mind, so she could go home and … and … she didn't know what. Right now, she simply had to sleep.

The sounds of the front door closing and Poppy calling, 'Mrs Mudgely, where are you? Mrs Mudgely, hello-ooo,' woke Jane. The cat jumped off the bed and when Jane emerged, Poppy was sitting in an armchair, nuzzling the cat's back, her bag, jacket and keys in a pile on the floor. Poppy started, then attempted a smile.

'Hi, I didn't realise you were in. I've had a bit of a tough day.'

Jane wanted to hug her, but pulled a dining-chair over and sat close by.

'What happened? Do you want to talk about it.'

Poppy brushed tears away with the back of her hand. 'One of the girls in my class came to school today with bruises on her legs,' she said. 'When I put my hand on her shoulder and asked her what had happened she flinched and it turns out she's got bruises all down her back too. All she would say was, "Mum got drunk and I dropped a plate." So social welfare is involved now, and the girl is frightened she will be sent away. Some of the other kids were upset and unsettled, too, and one of the boys started bragging about how much he could take "without blubbing". Of course, I managed it all, but I do hate it. I just can't understand how people can hit children, it upsets me terribly. Sorry.' She clasped the hand on her shoulder for a moment.

'Can I make you some coffee? Or tea?'

'Actually, what I really feel like is a beer. There are some in the bottom of the fridge. Will you join me?'

'Sure.' Beer in the afternoon, very cold beer Jane discovered, was a new experience she did not mind at all.

'I'm okay now. Thanks,' said Poppy, with a full smile this time. 'I should be used to it by now, it happens one way or another most years, but it always upsets me, especially when the child feels they have done something bad or they're being punished. Marie is such a quiet girl, I can't imagine anyone getting angry with her, let alone angry enough to hit her. This stuff has got a lot to answer for.' She held up the can.

'It is not the can that hit the child. Sorry. That was preachy.'

'That's okay; you're right, of course, I just wish every child could have a decent childhood, you know. Silly really, it should be so simple and it's actually so hard. Anyway, how was your first day at the museum?'

'Half-day in fact. I've been asleep all afternoon.'

The conversation made its way around to Jane's plans. She had woken from her nap certain about what she wanted.

'If you are really sure it will not inconvenience you, I would like to stay here,' she said to Poppy, 'as long as you will let me pay rent and a share of the phone and power and grocery shopping.'

'Yes!' said Poppy, 'Or no, it wouldn't inconvenience me. And I was going to point out that if you stayed in Birkenhead you would be very dependent on Peter thingy for transport. It's very nice over there, but quite cut off if you don't have a car. Has anyone told you about Auckland's rotten public transport yet? I would like you to stay, but no rent. You can help with the power and phone and groceries but no rent. George told me you didn't have much of a budget and I don't need rent, I earn a good salary.' Rose's voice chipped in with, 'You could have an even better salary if you weren't so stubborn about being a classroom teacher and went for a senior job.'

'I'm okay for money, I live pretty cheaply, I like it that way, and I really don't want any rent from you.'

Jane conceded on the rent and insisted on paying for all the groceries they went out for, including two bottles of New Zealand wine. When they returned Martia and Eve were sitting on the front steps chatting. 'We've been plotting for the Rape Crisis Collective meeting later,' explained Eve, 'and had an hour to spare and thought we would come and welcome Jane to New Zealand.' She held out her hand to the Englishwoman and names were exchanged. 'Came to check her out more likely,' thought Poppy as they went inside.

They did not accept Poppy's offer to join them for tea, confusing Jane who had planned to make 'supper', so they spent some entertaining moments comparing English-English with New

Zealand-English, then gave Jane her first lessons in Maori pronunciation, beginning with 'Maungawhau' and 'Aotearoa.' She excused herself and came back with a notebook.

'There is so much that is new, I will not remember half of it unless I write it down,' she answered their amusement. 'And there's "Te Papa …"' putting the accent on 'Te', which resulted in a lesson from Eve about even emphasis in Maori syllables …

'Except when they're long,' interrupted Martia. 'And by the way, have you noticed yet that the Auckland Museum people don't like the Te Papa lot?'

'I did wonder a little, at the meeting this morning. It seemed that there are some political disputes …'

'That's putting it mildly. They hate each other.'

'Oh, come on,' Eve interrupted this time. 'It's just sibling rivalry,' she said to an increasingly bewildered Jane, 'you know, competing for mummy government's attention and more spending money.'

Putting away the shopping after Martia and Eve had left for their meeting and giving Jane a tour of the kitchen cupboards and drawers, Poppy asked her if she had an internet email address, and would she like to check it on Poppy's computer.

'Thank you, yes to both. But first I would like to cook my famous spaghetti bolognaise. Out, please,' and she made as if to shoo Poppy out of the kitchen.

'Okay, I'll go quietly.'

After a companionable meal, where Poppy talked about the on-going drama of Amelia and Tony, two colleagues having an affair with each other, she asked about the project that had brought Jane to New Zealand.

Jane told her about the significant bequest from a patron who, 'made his money in chemicals. He had no family and left half his fortune to the museum and the other half to the clean-up and development project around the river Tees – which, of course, his factories had helped pollute.' It had taken two years for the decision to be made that the bequest would be used to refurbish the museum's public display areas and make them more 'modern and interactive'. This had led to the decision to send someone to New Zealand to study developments at the Auckland Museum and at the national museum, Te Papa Tongarewa.

'At first the board chairman was going to come but a group of board members and staff argued for a professional and it ended up being me,' Jane explained. Poppy nodded sympathetically as Jane told her about the unpleasantness that had gone on for a time over the final decision to send her, the longest-serving curator. 'We really are very small in museum terms,' she went on, 'and there is only one other full curator and he is new.' Jane talked also about her sense of responsibility to learn as much as she could and report back fully. 'And then there will be all the politics around deciding what we can actually do with the money we have. I am not looking forward to that part.'

'I can relate to that,' responded Poppy, 'that's why I've never gone for a big-C Career in education. I like being in the classroom and I don't like all the pushing and shoving that goes on when you get to be in charge of other people. I'm happy being a teacher, and I'm glad I never let anyone talk me into anything different. Katrina – my mother – certainly tried. She's ambitious, she was deputy CEO of the National Qualifications Authority when she retired, about five years ago now, and then she went straight onto all sorts of committees. Now she's National President of the Heart and Respiratory Foundation but she's given up on me. She says I'm "just like George, no drive," and she's probably right, and I don't mind. How is George, anyway?'

Jane smiled. 'I like George a lot. He's very easy to work with, though he'd rather work with his trichoptera than anything else. Actually, that's not quite true any more, he has branched out into lepidoptera as well. I think he was pleased to give up on beetles and bees and ants when he retired, not that he works many less hours now – he, he comes in nearly every day. Do you know he's considered a world expert on trichoptera? And he's getting a name for his inventiveness too. He designed a different way of assembling trays that makes them more effective for keeping out impurities, and now he has invented a pin that works without piercing the insects' bodies, it has this little gripper part at the top. It will be a bit more expensive to make, but worth it for the lack of damage to specimens. Oh dear, am I telling you more than you want to know?'

'Not at all. It's great to hear about my father and what he's doing. He never says much about his work.'

'Are you following the America's Cup races? No, it is still the Louis Vuitton Challenger's Cup, I believe.'

Poppy was startled at the sudden change of topic. 'No. Only to curse at the traffic. I don't like sailing.'

'Oh, there's that photo of you and someone in the dining room, with a yacht in the background, so I thought ...'

'That's Kate who used to be my partner. She loved sailing.'

'I see. Was it the difference about sailing that led you to separate?' Jane was startled at herself asking such a bold question.

Poppy made herself keep breathing and the world around and within her froze for only a few seconds.

'Are you all right? Your face has gone all white. Look, I should not have asked, I apologise, I am sorry I asked, I was being inquisitive, I should not have been so insensitive.' Jane was flustered.

'It's all right, it was a long time ago,' Poppy said as soon as she could speak.

'I would like to hear what happened, if you are willing to tell me. But, of course, if you would rather not say, that is completely all right. Oh dear, I have done this all wrong.'

Poppy shrugged. 'No you haven't. If I don't want people to ask I can put the photo away. There's not much to tell, really. It's a long time ago and ages since I talked to anyone about it.'

Mrs Mudgely cocked one ear, with a quizzical, and possibly approving, look.

8

1990

The wind was gusty as Poppy walked home from school. She was nearly at her gate when Eve pulled up at the curb and wound down the passenger-side window. 'Hi there. I was just about to drop by to see whether you and Kate would like to come to an impromptu Valentine's Day party tonight at our place. BYO everything except the candles and romantic music – any time from eight.'

'Thanks Eve, but Kate's arranging a romantic dinner out somewhere. We could drop in later maybe, though she's on day shift and has to be at the hospital at seven so I won't promise.'

'Be good to see you if you make it, give Kate a Valentine hug from me if you don't.' And Eve drove off.

Poppy was sitting on the front step in the sun reading the paper, waiting for Kate to return from sailing, when the phone rang. At first she couldn't make out who it was, and was just about deciding it was kids on an after-school prank, when she heard, 'Kate ... Kate is ...' and recognised Belinda's voice, sobbingly incoherent.

'Kate! What about Kate? Is she there?' Poppy asked, her stomach in her throat. There was another voice in the background, 'Stupid woman, I said not yet ...' And Bob was on the phone with none of his usual heartiness. 'There's been a bit of a problem with Kate's yacht, probably nothing to worry about.'

'Where's Kate?' Poppy's voice was a squeak.

'Look, don't worry. She and the boat are still out in the harbour, a capsize apparently, and the coastguard is there. I'll ring you back when I know more, I'm sorry that stupid woman got on the phone.'

'No. She wasn't stupid. She was right. Someone should have rung me right away.' Poppy took a deep breath, and said, 'I'm coming over, right now,' putting the phone down before he could answer and frantically looking for her keys, which were by the phone. When did she last drive her car? One week ago? Two weeks? Would it start? Oh, please God it would start. It was more than three weeks. The battery would be flat, the jumper leads were in Kate's car …

Breathing fast, she dialled Martia's number. 'Martia, it's Poppy, something's happened …'

'Hiya, I was just going to ring you about Eve's toni…'

'Martia, listen. Something has happened to Kate, out on the harbour. Will you drive me to the North Shore? Please, Martia, I don't think my car will start.'

'What's happened? No, never mind, I'll be there in ten minutes.'

Poppy was on the footpath when Martia drew up and in the car almost before it stopped.

'North Shore, right? Where?' Martia had already turned into Mt Eden Road and was heading for the motorway on-ramp. Never mind if Poppy hadn't locked the door or had left something on the stove, she'd ring someone as soon as she got a chance and ask them to go and check. Poppy was ashen. Martia felt a rush of gratitude for the training and experience of ten years as a volunteer at Rape Crisis.

'Bayswater.'

'What's happened?'

'I don't know. Belinda, Kate's mother rang, drunk I think and crying and I couldn't understand what she was saying, and her father came on and said Kate's yacht had capsized and Kate was, I don't know, still out there, still out on the water and the coast guard was there.' Poppy took a big gulp of air. 'She knows what to do when the boat capsizes, it's happened to her lots, she likes to make it go as fast as she can, that's why she called this one *Swift*. Bob said not to worry but he sounded worried. He said he'd ring back when he knew more but I couldn't stay there waiting, I just couldn't. I don't even know where she's booked us for dinner.' Poppy stopped and stared grimly at the slow-moving cars in front of them, willing them to hurry, hurry, hurry.

'I'm glad you rang me.' Martia put her hand on Poppy's knee for a moment then concentrated on choosing the fastest-moving lane onto the Harbour Bridge. Poppy sat silently, her body clenched.

'Breathe, Poppy, breathe,' said Martia.

'Oh. Yes. I was thinking about when I was a kid and if I held my breath until, I dunno, some landmark George chose, then whatever I wished would come true. She's all right, when we get there she'll be all right and tell me I was silly, she will, won't she?'

'I don't know Poppy, I certainly hope so.' Martia changed lanes again, ready for the exit. Once they were off the bridge the traffic was heavy, but blessedly moving. Turning into Bayswater Road, Martia asked for more instructions. Neither had said anything for ten minutes.

Poppy saw every house, every tree, every power pole with utter clarity, as though she were swooping up to each one and taking finely focused glossy photographs. Photographs with no people in them. She felt nothing. It was as though her skin had turned to glass.

There were three cars outside the Smiths' house. One was Kate's, and one a police car. Poppy let out a sound that raised goosebumps on Martia's skin and was heading down the path to the front door before the ignition was turned off, calling, 'Kate! Kate! Ka–ate!'

Minutes later, having made one garbled phone call to Eve that she hoped had made enough sense, including reminding her where Poppy kept a door key hidden outside, Martia was sitting on the sofa with her arms around a sobbing Poppy, and the story had emerged.

A man in a fourth-floor apartment in St Heliers had spotted the yacht on its side, the sail and the centre-board on the water, through his binoculars. He had carried on with his regular early evening sweep of the harbour and, when he came back to that spot a few minutes later nothing had changed, so he rang 111 and the coastguard launch went out. The fact that he could make out the identification number on the sail meant that, by the time the police launch reached the yacht, they knew who owned it. They were taking Kate's body to the morgue.

'Didn't they try and resuscitate her? Why didn't they bring her round? Did anyone try? Why didn't you ring me? I'm her partner!' the words came fast, Poppy's voice high and shaky, her eyes darting from the policeman to Bob and back again. The policeman went slightly red. He looked at Bob Smith for help and got none. 'The address on the registration was this one miss, and my sergeant knows the place, lives down the road, knows Mr and Mrs Smith ...'

Poppy shrugged and subsided. Hearing what had happened mattered more than anything else right now. Kate had been trapped under the sail. She might have been hit on the head by the boom. 'Never!' thought Poppy without saying anything, 'not with the way she moved on the boat.' And one arm had apparently been tangled in the starboard sheet.

Belinda was huddled in one of the big chairs that matched the sofa, her arms folded tightly across her chest, making small mewling sounds, a policewoman trying ineffectually to comfort her. A police-man, Bob, and the other man, suited, his hands folded in front of him whenever he was not talking, were talking quietly together. The third man was clearly an undertaker. ('Faster to the scene than a towey to a car smash,' thought Martia, then chided herself; of course, Bob would have rung him. 'When exactly,' she wondered, 'would he have deemed it the right time to ring Poppy?')

Poppy's sobs had subsided. Words drifted over from the three men. 'Arrangements', 'autopsy', and 'identification' were three Martia picked up. Poppy sprang up with such unexpected force that Martia fell back into the sofa while Poppy marched the four steps to the trio of men. Her face was white and wet with tears. She stood eye-to-eye with Bob Smith. 'If I was a man I would be married to Kate and you would expect me to take part in the arrangements. She is – was – my partner for thirteen years and you are not going to do this, this "arranging" as you call it without me. I don't even know where she – her body – is.' Poppy's voice was firm but her hands fluttered and Martia thought she was waving slightly on her feet. The policeman saw it too and put out his hand towards her. Martia stood up, and went to stand close beside her friend. Poppy's hand grasped hers so fiercely she winced. 'Please let me do the right thing,' she said to herself and spoke to the policeman.

'Tell us where Kate is and exactly what happens now,' Martia said.

The policeman looked dubiously at Bob, who looked around the room, clearly at a loss. When his eyes came to Poppy's face he hesitated for a moment, then nodded to the policeman.

'Well, Miss …'

'My name is Poppy Sinclair. Please call me Poppy, or Ms, I am not a child.'

'Well, ah, Poppy, Miss, um Ms Smith's body will be at the – ah – morgue by now awaiting formal identification by her father – or, or – someone. There will be an autopsy, probably tomorrow and if there is no reason to not release the body the undertaker will make arrangements with you,' – he looked from Poppy to Bob and back again, '– and the incident will go to the coroner. There will have to be a coroner's report and perhaps a hearing.'

'What happens when the body goes to you?' Martia talked directly to the undertaker. He unfolded his hands.

'We do the – uh – the embalming,' he said, 'then she will be in our very nice reception room, where people might want to come and pay their last respects …' He broke off at Poppy's choked, 'No!'

'She's right. Kate's body must go home, to the home she and Poppy shared.' Everyone swung around to Katrina, standing in the doorway.

As she walked into the room Poppy threw herself into her mother's arms and sobbed. Katrina hugged her for a moment, patted her back and passed her back to Martia with a nod. Martia acquiesced, comforting her friend while she listened.

Katrina approached Bob, holding out her hand so he had no option but to shake it. 'Do you know what ha...?' he began. 'I know enough,' Katrina cut him off. 'I know there was an accident on the water and now I know Kate is dead.' She looked at the undertaker. 'Terrible, terrible.' She patted the back of Bob's hand. 'Thank heavens Poppy's friend had the sense to let me know something dreadful had happened and where you all were.'

'Yes!' thought Martia, who hadn't even thought to tell Eve to ring Katrina. She didn't know Katrina's surname herself, so how did Eve find her?

No-one had noticed Belinda and the policewoman leave the room. When they returned Belinda showed no surprise at seeing Katrina. The policewoman put a large tray carrying bone china mugs and a large silver teapot with matching milk jug and sugar bowl on the dining-table and Belinda sat down and started pouring tea. Martia added two spoons of sugar to one and handed it to Poppy, who grimaced at the first sweet taste but held it in both hands as if to warm them and kept sipping. Belinda handed cups around. Katrina waved the tea away. She took Bob by the arm and led him to the far wall and turned him so they stood side-by-side facing the room.

'Poppy and Bob and Belinda at least, all need to see her, to see Kate's body as soon as possible,' Katrina announced. 'I know that much from John's family.' And so it was arranged. They would all go to the morgue. Poppy and Bob would do the formal identification. Belinda and Katrina would follow the police car and Martia would follow them.

'Her mother is in no state ...' began Bob.

'I must see her!' Belinda was on her feet, steadying herself with one hand on the table, tears running down her face, her make-up smeared. The policewoman took her other elbow. Katrina got two business cards from the undertaker and handed one to Martia. 'Let me organise this man, dear,' she said to Poppy, 'I know the senior partner in his firm. You do want Kate at home, don't you?' Poppy nodded vigorously. 'Good. We'll have to make some decisions about the funeral too but we won't be able to set a day until the coroner releases the body. I suppose there will be an inquest.'

'It is usual, madam, in cases of sudden death. However, the North Shore coroner is considerate and will no doubt expedite matters with his usual efficiency. I will call on you in the morning madam.'

'At this address,' and Katrina wrote Poppy's address on the back of one of her own cards and handed it to him. 'Nine o'clock. Now, we'll all go to Poppy and Kate's from the morgue tonight. If you drop Bob and Belinda there, I'll run them home.' This to the policewoman, who was holding car keys. Bob made as though to object, then subsided.

Martia realised they had been in the Smiths' house for little over an hour. She felt a hand on her arm. It was Belinda pointing at Kate's shoulder bag on the floor by the French doors. 'Thank you,' mouthed Martia, slinging it onto her shoulder, hoping that anyone who noticed would think it was hers. She picked up her own backpack from the hallway and hurried out to her car, concerned to not miss the convoy to the morgue.

As Poppy looked down at Kate's still, still face all her surroundings disappeared. There was just her and Kate and the cold. She put her hand on Kate's clammy arm – this, of all things, convinced her this was a dead body, not her Kate; Kate's skin was never clammy in life. The cold and the stillness seeped into Poppy through her hand along her arm into her organs and her bones, forcing out all feeling, all vitality. She turned away only in response to the pressure of Martia's hand gently leading her to the door, keeping her eyes on the still, dead face until the last possible moment. As the door closed behind them, Poppy felt Martia crying and was startled. Of course, Kate had been her friend. Bob looked old. Belinda clung to his arm.

All the lights were on in the Grey Lynn flat. Eve was there, and Bessie. Alexa was talking on the phone. 'Eve! Your party! We didn't ...'

'Oh Poppy, Poppy, a party couldn't matter less right now, I am so sorry, so, so sorry.' They hugged each other as the rest of the group entered the room. Alexa finished on the phone. 'I've left a message on the school answer-phone that Poppy won't be in tomorrow,' she said. Katrina acknowledged Poppy's friends, introduced Bob and Belinda, looked questioningly at Poppy, who nodded, and took command again.

'How did you know her number?' Martia mouthed to Eve, indicating Katrina. Eve pointed to the flip-up address book by the phone. 'Under K,' she mouthed back. So Eve had come round straight after she got the phone call. Martia guessed that Bessie and Alexa had already arrived to help prepare for the party and that Eve's partner had stayed with the rest of the guests.

'Poppy, what would Kate want by way of a funeral?' Poppy stared at Katrina wordlessly, tears welling.

'Can't this wait, the girl's clearly too upset.' Bob was gruff.

'If we wait, you will go ahead and do something entirely inappropriate, and she is not a girl.'

Poppy couldn't help herself, she giggled.

'You see, she's hysterical, she needs a doctor.' Bob looked around for support and again found none. Belinda was staring at the floor.

'I'm not hysterical and she's right, I'm not a girl. Kate would want, and I want something simple, no church, no minister, no god.'

'Poppy,' Alexa's voice was tentative, 'I think all of us, Kate's and your friends, and you, and her parents, of course, we could all work something out.'

And over the next twenty-four hours they did. Bob struggled with not being in charge and when his offer to pay for catering was turned down in favour of Kate's friends doing the food, he more or less gave

89

up. The women were careful to keep telling him the plans and asking his opinion but once he had found a way to tell his colleagues and golfing friends that, 'the women are making the arrangements, and I decided to leave them to it, gives them something to do,' he stopped ringing every couple of hours.

Belinda wanted the song 'What is Life' from the Gluck opera *Orpheus and Eurydice* to be included in the service and brought over the CD then stayed all morning, doing the dishes, a load of washing and some vacuuming. Katrina was dealing with the undertaker and the coroner, trying to find out when the body would be released and a date for an inquest; she also rang George in England and did not encourage him to come over. 'You can do your bit when I get her to go away. That might not be for a while, but she will,' she told him.

Martia spent all day Thursday on the phone. 'I knew there was a reason why I don't have a real job,' she said to no-one in particular. Eve visited Poppy's principal and he asked to be informed of the date of the funeral and implied that he thought a week off should be long enough. Bob went to the hospital and spoke to the chief nurse. People came to the house with food, flowers, their own grief and a real desire to help. Poppy was never alone; Martia stayed the first night, May-Yun the second and third.

Alexa and Bessie had taken charge of planning the ceremony, and they would conduct it together. At Poppy's suggestion they had rung the number on the door of the hall down the road that used to be a Masonic Lodge and had been sold to the local Anglican Church. It was bare, but it had chairs and a basic sound system, and a kitchen and they could have it for Monday but not Saturday. They booked it for all day Monday, Katrina having told them not to worry about the cost of anything and after a consultation with each other they agreed to take her at her word. 'What a difference access to money makes at a time like this,' commented Bessie, thinking of her mother's funeral when she was eighteen and it took her and her brother a year to pay off the undertaker.

'Bob will be offended, if he knows we have taken money from Katrina and not from him,' Alexa worried. The others nodded, and then did nothing further about it.

May-Yun was the most successful at getting Poppy to eat and drink. She would sit quietly stroking her arm or her hair, offering bits of food, sips of orange or tea, crooning sometimes, talking quietly about Kate a little, often silent. When Stefan came by with the children after school on Friday, they all piled onto the sofa with Poppy. Ivan sat on her lap and snuggled into her. Led by Annie they had made a card. After a few minutes Annie and Chan got involved with helping to make purple and silver wreaths for the hall.

Just before five o'clock, Katrina rang to say that Kate's body had gone to the undertaker's for embalming and would be at the house about eleven the next day. The cause of death was 'accidental, by drowning,' she reported. Stefan had answered the phone. 'How is everything?' his mother asked him.

'Under control in a chaotic sort of way, I think. Poppy looks dreadful, white as a ghost, and red-eyed. It's like everything is going on around her, and people talk to her and sit with her, and she's not really there, she's gone off somewhere inside herself. She won't have a doctor or any sleeping pills or anything and May-Yun says that's best, so I don't push her. I tend to trust May-Yun's opinion on these things. The kids want to be here for a bit so I think I'll go outside and mow the lawns. I seem to remember that Poppy has a push mower some-where.'

'I'm not worried about Poppy, Stefan. George's mother did that when his father died. He went and stayed with her and saw her through all the arrangements and the funeral and he said she was walking and talking but not really there in some way he couldn't describe and he used the same words you did, "she's gone off to some place inside herself". On the morning of the fifth day after he died, she had clearly "come back" and she sent George away. It will be harder for Poppy, this is so sudden and Kate was so young ... but she's got all the support and care in the world. I absolutely agree with May-Yun that drugging her is not going to help in the long run. Belinda is doing enough of that for both of them.'

'What?'

'You don't need to tell this to Poppy but I have had two maudlin, drunken phone calls from Belinda saying it's all her fault, she killed Kate because when Kate came in to go sailing they had a drink together – a small whisky she said, but I've seen the way she pours small whiskies – Kate had had a bad day at work – and then they had an argument and Kate stormed out and went sailing so Belinda has convinced herself it was all her fault. The second time she rang I was a mite impatient, well, very impatient really. I told her to pull herself together and be sure she didn't burden Poppy with any of this. You might tell someone that she's sorting out some photos of Kate when she was young ... you know, celebrating the life of kind of thing, and is expecting to bring them over for the funeral. I don't think she's told anyone what's she doing. Are they calling it a funeral, by the way?'

'I don't think so.' Stefan wasn't certain about anything. 'Ceremony, is what they mostly say. Bob seems to have fallen out of the picture altogether, Martia says if he's not in charge he doesn't know how to take part at all, and she's concerned that he may not show at the funer... ceremony, which would be awful for Belinda apart from anything else.'

'He'll be there. And Belinda too, a sober Belinda if I can manage it. That would have been easier if the funeral were earlier in the day.'

'Two o'clock seemed a good idea to me, then people can go to work in the morning. A couple of the women here have already taken these two days off I gather. May-Yun wants the children to come, but I'm not sure about Ivan.'

'Take all the children. It might be hard for them at the time but it's better. If something happens to you or May-Yun they are much better equipped to deal with it. Believe me.'

There was no way Stefan was going to oppose the combination of his wife and his mother. May-Yun wanted him to bring the children back in the morning so they would be there when Kate's body arrived. He was shocked, but allowed himself to be persuaded. It helped when May-Yun suggested he could drop them off and go into work; the building supply warehouse he managed had its summer sale starting. When he told Poppy about Belinda and the photos, Poppy said she and May-Yun had just been talking about that, about photos, and she had decided to do some for the hall and some for the house, so Belinda's could be part of both.

'How will you put them up?' asked Stefan, and was absurdly pleased when he was able to offer some board from his work that would do the job, and they talked about sizes and shapes, and he went off to cut the grass, with a note in his pocket about what to bring the next morning. He was not so happy about Poppy ringing Belinda to talk about the photos in view of what Katrina had just told him, and tried to make an opportunity to tell this to May-Yun but Poppy was on the phone before he could do it. May-Yun told him later that Belinda had been thrilled to be asked to take part in arranging the photos and was bringing hers over in the morning, so she would be there when Kate's body arrived. Stefan allowed himself a little guilty relief that he wouldn't be present and acknowledged to himself as he pushed the mower up and down the back garden, that he was slightly envious too, of the women and their ability to take such emotional occasions front on, without ducking and diving behind the professionals, the doctors and undertakers. 'Do it yourself,' was a phrase he understood in relation to working on a property, here it was being applied to life and death; he had never before been so aware of how closely the two were connected.

When the hearse arrived, at exactly eleven on Saturday morning, there were ten women (Poppy, Martia, May-Yun, Alexa and Bessie, Eve and her partner Shirley, Katrina, Belinda, and Rina) and three children (Annie – who at thirteen would object to being called a child – Chan and Ivan) at the house. They had already discussed who would carry Kate in.

Katrina was gratified to see that the senior partner at the undertakers, Stuart McKennan, an acquaintance of hers from the council's Community Board, had accompanied the hearse driver. He was much more practised than the younger man, whose name she could never remember, at maintaining an impassive demeanour in what were undoubtedly unusual circumstances.

Martia, Alexa, Bessie, Eve, Shirley and Rina carried in the closed coffin and carefully place it to one side of the double bed. Katrina motioned for it to be opened. Poppy, May-Yun, Belinda and Katrina watched. It was not until she went up to stand beside the bed that Poppy saw Kate's face again. She was trembling. The others stood back. Ivan held tightly to his mother's hand. Kate's face was recognisably hers but drained of any colour of life, pale and absolutely still, with a slight bruise near the left temple. Her hands, unnaturally white, were folded on her chest.

'She never lay neat and tidy like that when she was alive, she spread all over the place,' Poppy's voice was flat and expressionless and she was stroking Kate's hair and arm. 'Cold,' she said, and turned to face the others.

'Thank you,' she said. 'Thank you everyone for … for everything, everything.'

During the afternoon people came and went, including some of Kate's work colleagues Poppy had never met. She wondered for a moment how they knew, then recalled that for the last two days there had always been someone on the phone. Some who came didn't go into the bedroom at all, others had a quick glance at Kate's face and hurried out, yet others sat on the bed, stroked her head or arms or hands, talked to her. Poppy asked for some time alone with her and sat for thirty minutes, a hand cupping Kate's head, talking in a low voice, telling her about the arrangements and who was coming from out of town for Monday's ceremony and, at the end, how angry Poppy was at her for leaving her. Poppy talked about her anger in the same low, flat voice that had been hers since the evening of Valentine's Day. Then she walked out to the kitchen and said she wanted to make a banana cake for Monday, were there any bananas?

Stirring the mixture in a bowl she held under her left arm, Poppy walked into the bedroom and stood at the end of the coffin. 'This one's for you, babe,' she said, and scooped a generous dollop of mixture from the bowl to her own mouth. She made three banana cakes in all and eventually fell asleep on the bed beside the coffin and slept for five hours. When she woke at four a.m. May-Yun was snoring quietly on a pile of cushions on the floor at the end of the bed. Poppy crept past her to the hallway and very carefully and quietly opened the front door.

Sitting on the step in the warm, moist night air, she felt a cold fog of misery fold around her and hugged it to herself. 'This is what I have of Kate now,' she thought, 'this feeling is mine, mine alone, this is what is left of the us that we were. As long as I can feel this I still have something of her.' There were no more tears.

9

1999

'I went back to school after a week, I couldn't bear not doing anything. D'you know what got me through the first few months?'

Jane shook her head.

'Friends, my friends. Katrina was great too, in her brisk way. Even Stefan. May-Yun changed over that time from being my sister-in-law to being my friend. They all got me through. Them and the therapist I saw for a bit during the first months when I was just hanging on. I really believed then that if I stopped feeling miserable I would be losing Kate altogether, that my misery kept her alive – in me, or for me, or something like that. I made myself a cocoon out of it, like one of George's trichoptera larvae, wrapped it around me, and tried to metamorphose into someone else who didn't feel anything new. I sort of did, in a way, and that's where the therapist was good, she encouraged me to have a cocoon and then to come out of it. She wouldn't have the idea of not feeling anything, though, insisted that feelings would be there anyway and I might as well know about them. I guess I'm pleased about that now.'

Jane's eyes were moist. 'I don't know what to say. That is such a tragic story. Parents dying is quite different, especially when they are old and sick.'

'I don't know what losing parents is like, yet. But that year, 1990, was the worst year of my life, at times I didn't think I would get through it, I thought I would die from the grief and the pain. I really had believed that Kate and I would grow old together ...' her voice tailed off.

'I am so sorry, Poppy.'

'Thanks. I'm okay these days, though I still freeze up when I think of Kate unexpectedly, and I – um – didn't deal with you having the same – actually it's not the same, it's similar but not the same. Colouring, that is. I've even been involved with someone else, not that it worked out. There's some permanent scar tissue maybe, but basically I'm in good working order.' Suddenly, Poppy stood up. 'And if I'm going to stay that way I had better get some sleep. Are you warm enough? It's not usually this cold in November, apparently there's an unusual weather pattern. Anyway, the weather was a lot better last month.'

'Yes, thank you, I am quite warm enough. It is hard to believe I am not going into winter like everyone at home. At home! Oh heavens! May I take you up on your offer of checking my email before I go to bed? Will that disturb you?'

'No. No, you won't disturb me. The computer is in the extra spare bedroom, sometimes glorified by the name of "office".' Poppy demonstrated turning on, booting up and logging on to her internet connection. 'Don't worry about how long you take, I never use all the time I pay for. I guess it's still pretty early for someone who slept for the afternoon. Joke. Tease,' she added, at Jane's look of consternation, and went off to bed wondering at herself. Mrs Mudgely followed.

As Poppy was getting undressed and sorting out clothes for the next day she thought out loud to the cat. 'Here I am teasing that serious Englishwoman, Mrs M, me, the one who so hates teasing. Not to mention telling her all about when Kate died. And I don't even feel bad now, in fact I feel positively good. What do you think about all this, Mrs M?' The cat stopped kneading a spot on the bed for a moment, looked at Poppy, then went back to her kneading. 'Okay, be phlegmatic. I didn't really want to know what you think, anyhow.' That was surely a small grunt as Mrs Mudgely lay down, not a harrumph. Poppy rummaged in her wardrobe. 'She still hasn't said a word about herself,' she muttered to a line of trousers, 'but I reckon there's a significant other waiting on a message from her, and I reckon that significant other is a woman.'

In the next room Jane was staring at the computer screen. There was a message from Héloise. She scanned the email again,

… that's why we set up the phone card, so you could call … you knew I would be out … you must be having such a wonderful time … keeping the home fires burning … missing you … we didn't decide on colours for the guest room before you left, what do you think about a pale yellow? … it's cold and grey … Benjy is sulking because you haven't called or written … May and June (May actually) are finally pregnant, they are so thrilled and happy and full of plans … lonely without you … have you found out what you will do to keep in contact if the Y2K meltdown happens … I am really not looking forward to winter on my own …

A heavy tiredness settled over Jane. She started her reply:

My darling Héloise.

Then stopped and stared at the words. Did she mean them? Of course she did!

I am sorry you have not heard more from me. It was more difficult than I anticipated while I was travelling and I arrived very jetlagged and not functioning very well. I am going to stay here at Poppy's house – you remember, you met her father, George, he works with me …

When she had finished, Jane read through what she had written. It seemed forced so she changed a few words, added a line and her name, then remembered they always ended phone calls and emails with 'I love you' so put that in before her name, feeling vaguely guilty that she wasn't sure she felt it, and sent the message.

Over the next few days Poppy and Jane developed some ease in their comings and goings and, at the same time, saw little of each other. Museum colleagues invited Jane to their houses and their after-work drinks and one took her for a twilight drive around the waterfront to a restaurant in St Heliers for a dinner that she thought was expensive and that he insisted on paying for. His partner had met them at the restaurant, which was near their home, and Jane insisted in turn on getting herself a taxi back to Mt Eden. She had been given a desk and access to a shared computer at the museum and open entry to all its sections. By the end of her third day she had made a detailed plan for the rest of her four weeks at the Auckland Museum; on 5 December she would go to Wellington for a fortnight, then she had six weeks holiday before she returned home.

What it meant for it to be a 'War Memorial' Museum had become a lot clearer to her, and she understood the choice of site on top of the rise in the domain very clearly each morning as she walked up the hill to the side entrance of the imposing building. There was so much to take in, so much that she had read about that was being put into practice, it was overwhelming. She could only deal with it by making detailed notes and taking photos and organising them into folders at the end of each day.

The Matapuna Natural History Information Centre was exactly what she wanted at The Cleveland. The maps, posters, photographs, CD-ROMs, video viewing rooms – they all made the material so exciting. In the main display areas simple things like terns 'flying' above the mock-up of a seashore were inspiring. And setting up the seashore in its huge glass-covered case, in the centre of a space so visitors could walk around it, was something she would never have thought of. The trays of specimens, so important to students and scholars, were still available, just not so centrally positioned. The birds mounted on racks and information pamphlets at The Cleveland that she had been so proud of seemed lack-lustre and dated. It had been a good decision to arrange for longer in

Auckland, she thought, because here it was more of a local museum, whereas Te Papa (she thought she could now say it with equal emphasis on all three syllables, though she doubted she would achieve Maori vowels without an English accent) was a national centre, on a scale far, far beyond a provincial museum like the one that had sent her here. Often she felt dizzy at the combination of impressions, technical information and excitement; this trip was certainly jolting her out of her comfortable work groove.

Poppy was pleased with herself for deciding to have Jane stay. Sharing the house had become relaxed, and it was a bonus to be able to email George and have him pleased with himself; he loved it when his machinations into the lives of his children were successful. The rush of drop-ins and phone calls from her friends she knew was curiosity – possibly even with a match-making edge for the incorrigible – with a big dollop of care and concern for her. She could imagine them. 'Who is she, anyway, this woman staying with Poppy?' 'Is she a lesbian?' 'Has she got a partner?' 'How long is she here for?' 'Why didn't we know about her?' Poppy was aware that she herself assumed that Jane was a lesbian, so far without any tangible evidence either way.

Saturday morning was overcast and showery. 'Pretty normal Auckland weather,' Poppy told Jane over a late breakfast. The scrambled eggs Jane had boasted about when she first arrived were indeed very good, as was the coffee and the perfect evenly-brown toast. There was a jar of honeysuckle flowers on the table, and Poppy's best blue and white china, which she couldn't remember having used at breakfast time before. Mrs Mudgely was under the table washing herself, interrupting her ablutions to lick up the occasional crumb from the floor. 'It's the butter she likes, really.' Poppy commented. 'She ate nearly half a block that I left on the bench once. I think she was sick, but she went outside and I wasn't certain.' By the time the story ended Mrs Mudgely had turned around so that her back was towards Poppy and was rubbing her head against Jane's legs.

'If you don't have other plans for today,' said Poppy, searching with her knife for a whole strawberry in the jam, 'I could take you on a scenic tour. You get a great view of the harbour and this side of the city from Mt Victoria in Devonport – we could get a ferry over and back and walk up if you like – and then we could drive around the waterfront, it looks quite different in the middle of the day, the colours are brilliant and the water sparkles – that's what Waitemata means, sparkling water – that's if the cloud lifts, and then drive across the city to Howick and you could meet my brother and his family, I'm sure George has told you all about them.'

'That sounds wonderful, but you must have things to do for yourself on a Saturday.'

'Well, I could vacuum, wash windows, clean out the garden shed, cut back the honeysuckle,' she smiled at the posy then at Jane, 'mow the lawn, do some planning for school, or catch up on my email, but I would rather play tour guide. Oh, and I'm going to a friend's birthday party tonight, it's Rina's fortieth, should be fun, her family will be there and her friends, she's got a big family and heaps of friends. She was one of the people who rallied around when Kate died. Would you like to come? I'm sure it would be fine, but I could give her a ring and check it out if you like. Hey, what's up? It's a party I've asked you to, not a wake.' There were tears in Jane's eyes.

'Sorry. I am overwhelmed by the kindness and generosity of everyone. Things were difficult at home before I left and it was all grey and getting wintry and now I'm here in spring, and everyone is so cheerful and so kind, I can hardly take it all in.' Poppy was nodding. Jane continued, 'I already turned down an offer of a day out at Waiuku and some horse-riding, on the grounds that I needed to write up my notes, so I probably should say no, but I would love to go driving with you. I am not sure about the party though, there's something about big parties and, well, I will not know anyone ...'

'Well, you've met both Martia and Eve, and I hear you made quite an impression on Bessie and Alexa on Wednesday when they called in before I got home. Anyway, no pressure.'

'Actually, I would like to see the city from the other side …'

Poppy jumped up, put her feet together, and bowed slightly from the waist. 'Your, ah, coach, madam, will depart from the front gate in thirty minutes. Sandwiches and cold beer will be part of the service.' Sitting down again, she said, 'You said things were difficult at home – do you want to talk about it?'

'Not really, not just now. Maybe some other time. See you at the coach.'

When Jane was back in her room she sat on the side of the bed and blew her nose then piled the papers she had spread out on the bed into one heap, alternate sections neat-edged and at right angles to each other. Tomorrow, or maybe tonight while Poppy was out at the party, she would send her first email report to the museum chairman, and phone Héloïse.

'See all those yachts and people over there, that's the America's Cup village.' Poppy was pointing as the ferry drew out into the harbour.

'Oh yes, I saw something about an Australian one sinking on the television news.'

'That was at the last challenge, somewhere in the States.'

'Really? And they still talking about it? I think I read something about a women's crew before I left home.'

'Yeah. You could be right.'

'Oh, look, that must be the sparkling water you were talking about. How do you say it again?' Jane was pointing to a patch of water where the sun was shining through a break in the clouds.

'Waitemata.' Poppy smiled as Jane practised earnestly, trying to say the Maori name of the harbour exactly as she had heard it.

Walking through the busy Devonport shops was slow, with Jane stopping and looking in the craft and second-hand shops. She offered to take the backpack carrying the cooler and picnic and Poppy agreed that she could take it on the way back to the ferry. Once past the shops, they strode up the road to the top of Mt Victoria, keeping pace with each other, stopping from time to time while Poppy pointed out landmarks. From the top of the hill, Auckland's volcanic cones were remarkable.

'There's Maungawhau, my house is on the right from here.' Poppy was pointing. 'The island over to the north-east is Rangitoto; One Tree Hill, is one of the most famous, the tree has been attacked recently, by a Maori protester, and is in bad shape apparently. There's Mt Roskill, and Panmure,' Poppy was gesturing and pointing.

'Tell me about Maori protests.'

'Oh my, that's a tall order. Let's get lunch first.'

Over ham and mustard sandwiches, with slices of tomato and cucumber and lettuce leaves on the side, accompanied by cold low-alcohol beer, Poppy talked about the Treaty of Waitangi, the Land Wars, the world wars, the urban migration, the Waitangi Tribunal and her own experiences of challenges from the anti-racism movement ('I hated it at the time, but they were right') and learning some ('very basic') Maori language.

'Rina knows a lot more than I do about all this. Her family is Maori but she was brought up Pakeha – as we say here – and got involved in the Bastion Point occupation.' Poppy pointed across the harbour to the headland that had been the site of the protest and subsequent police eviction and arrests more than twelve years earlier. 'Rina joined the occupation about halfway through,' she continued, 'more or less by chance, when she got involved with a Pakeha woman who was in one of the support groups. It really politicised her, and she has studied her whakapapa – that's like genealogy, but different too – and now she's involved with the Ngati Whatua – that's her iwi, or tribe, or one of them – claim at the Waitangi Tribunal. Whew! There's so much history and it's so complex. Maori are really tribal, you know, the idea of one homogenous group of Maori across the country is recent and not especially accurate.' Poppy stopped. 'I've got a few books you could read if you want to know more. It's not that I'm not willing to talk about this stuff, it's just that I'm not that well informed and I'm never sure I'll get it right.'

'I had no idea,' said Jane. 'My education about New Zealand, as far as it went, was clearly over-simplified and Anglophile. Captain Cook came from around Whitby where I grew up – there's a statue, and a museum.' Poppy was nodding; George had taken her around all the Cook memorials on her first visit to him in Middlesbrough. Jane went on, 'I think I arrived with vestiges of the "Little England" idea.' She looked at Poppy. 'I do appreciate you taking the trouble to educate me a little, I am more woefully ignorant than I had ever imagined.'

'That's okay.' Poppy grinned. 'I'm enjoying myself, it must be the teacher in me, even though I can't claim any expertise.'

Once they had packed the lunch things, Jane managed to get the pack onto her back first. They didn't talk much on their way back down the hill and through the town to the ferry. Jane stopped at one shop and bought a small bone spiral to send home to Héloise, knowing she was avoiding opportunities to talk about her partner, and feeling guilty and dishonest that she had been at Poppy's for nearly a week and not mentioned her. She resolved to make an opportunity before the end of the weekend.

By the time the ferry pulled in at the wharf in Auckland it was five o'clock. 'I think we might skip going to my brother's, it's later than I thought. Do you mind?' asked Poppy. 'If we go now we'll have to stay for dinner.'

'Aren't they expecting us?' Jane had become used to 'supper' being either 'tea' or 'dinner'.

'No, I thought we'd just call in, they're usually home on a Saturday afternoon, after about three. With Stefan's work and Ivan's sport, it's hard to get them Saturday morning.'

They were at the car and set off through heavy traffic for Poppy's house. When they arrived they pulled up behind a white Telstar. 'That looks like Katrina's car,' said Poppy, as her mother appeared down the steps. She waited while Poppy got out of the car and gave her a peck on the cheek. Katrina was dressed in grey silk. 'Classy and expensive,' thought Poppy.

'Thank heavens you're back,' Katrina was saying, 'I've an hour to wait before I meet Don in Newmarket for dinner with some overseas colleagues. I finished my shopping quicker than I thought – do you like my new shoes?' Katrina held out one foot, showing silver sandals. Poppy laughed. 'You know it's a waste of time showing me, a shoe is a shoe as far as I'm concerned. Here, meet Jane.

'How do you do.' Katrina shook hands. 'Poppy said you were coming, you're a colleague of her father's, aren't you? Nice to meet you.' She turned to Poppy, 'Are you going to offer your mother a drink?'

'Of course. Come on up. Beer, white wine, coffee, or I have some teabags.' Poppy led the way up the steps.

'A cup of tea would be lovely, dear.'

'Jane?'

'Another one of those cans of beer if you have one. Your cold beer is refreshing in this warmth.'

'If you call this warm, dear, you must be from England. Now tell me what has brought you here.'

Watching her mother making conversation with Jane, Poppy observed her skill with admiration and a little sadness. When she had returned from London in December 1991, three weeks after John Pomare's fatal heart attack, her mother had been different for a while. They had been housemates in Katrina's Herne Bay house for several months while Poppy did relief teaching and Katrina was clearly shaken by John's death and by the extent of her own grief. Gradually over the months, though, the brisk Katrina had returned. Since Don Smart came into her life she had become even more brittle, Poppy thought; she didn't like the 'Smart by name, smart by nature' Mr Business man, though he did seem genuinely fond of Katrina.

'Poppy, where are you? Earth to Poppy, come in dear.' That was a phrase George had used when she was a child; 'earth to Poppy, come in Poppy,' he would say when she was day-dreaming. She didn't like her mother using it, and she didn't like the familiar feeling that her mother was patronising her.

'Yes.'

'I was just saying to Jane that Don has a new launch. You should both come out on the harbour one day.'

'Not me, thanks, I like land under my feet, as you know, and I haven't been out on the harbour since …'

'I know dear, and it's time you did.'

'Please don't "know best" for me,' said Poppy, sitting down by her mother. 'I would much rather have a coffee with you than go out on Don's launch, but Jane might like it.' She looked across at her guest, who clearly did not know what to say. 'Sorry, Jane, I just threw you onto a cleft stick, there is no right answer, never mind, you don't have to give one.'

'I was talking to Stefan the other day,' said Katrina, abandoning any awkwardness, 'and he is concerned about Chan, he's not at all settled, and Stefan thinks he might not be being completely honest about what he is doing. Have you seen the boy lately?'

'What Chan needs,' said Poppy firmly, not mentioning his visit to her, 'is to be left alone to decide what he wants to do with his life and for Stefan to stop hounding him about careers and all that. What does May-Yun say?'

'I can't see Stefan hounding anyone, dear, he just has a parent's natural concern and, according to Stefan, May-Yun is as concerned as he is.'

Then Katrina decided she would drive her car home and take a taxi to Newmarket in case she had wine at dinner and didn't want to drive home. 'These business dinners can go on late, and it's easy to have another glass, and another. Which reminds me, I saw Belinda Smith the other day at a business cocktail party. I didn't have an opportunity to speak to her but she looked relatively sober when she left. Did you know her hair is completely grey?'

After she had waved Katrina goodbye, Poppy walked slowly back up the steps, thinking about Belinda, and whether to ring her, then making up her mind to see May-Yun soon, without Stefan if she could, maybe right after school, before he finished work, and ask her about Chan. The phone was ringing when she walked in the front door. She and May-Yun joked about how often one of them would ring when the other had been thinking of her. But the voice was not May-Yun's. It sounded upset and asked for Jane. Poppy took the cordless phone into the diningroom and handed it to Jane, who, as soon as she heard who it was, carried the phone into her room and quietly closed the door.

Taking the day's paper, Poppy went and sat on the front steps; time to start thinking about who to vote for in the elections in two weeks. She should have asked Katrina's opinion. No, she changed her mind rapidly, she was not at all sure she and Katrina would vote the same way these days.

As the sun dropped lower in the sky Poppy thought how odd it was to talk about the sun and rising and setting when actually it stayed put while the earth did all the moving. 'Knowing that the earth moves around the sun hasn't changed our way of thinking or our language,' her thoughts continued, 'I wonder if I could do something with that for science …?'

Jane sat down on the step beside her. 'I have to – no, I want to – tell you something,' she said.

'The woman on the phone?'

'Uh huh, Héloise.' Jane paused. Poppy waited silently. 'We've been partners since 1992. I was living with my mother who had emphysema that gradually got worse and worse. The last year there were nurses every day, but I lived in mother's house and organised everything. After Mother died Héloise and I rented a house together, then the owners wanted to sell so we bought it and we have lived there ever since. We got Benjy, he is a cocker spaniel, as soon as we moved in and he became the most loved and spoiled dog in England. I started at the Cleveland Museum in 1985 and, more than five years ago now, I was made curator and Héloise became public transport manager at the Council – she started as a bus driver, you know, and studied town planning and transport and worked her way up. She had left school at fifteen and worked in factories and shops.' Jane stopped for breath. She knew she was avoiding getting to the point. Poppy remained silent, watching the hills darken as they rolled away from the sun.

'Anyway,' Jane went on, 'we became very settled and domestic, socialising with friends and having holidays abroad and in the Lake District and everything was going along just fine until early last year, when Héloise decided – though she says she never decided, it just became something she had to do – she wanted to have a baby. No, she wanted us to have a baby; she would be the birth mother and I would be the other mother.

'At first I thought my resistance must be some kind of internalised prejudice about lesbians being parents. I have agonised, and thought, and read books, and been to a therapist, and I really do not want to have a child. My throat gets tight and I feel like I am being strangled when we talk about it, and she does not see that I am not being difficult, it is not a matter of her persuading or convincing me, I just cannot do it!' Jane was increasingly vehement. Poppy didn't speak, or look at her. Jane shrugged, and continued in her usual quiet voice. 'So things are strained. She was on the phone just now saying I should come home early, she is lonely and miserable and the thought of Christmas on her own is unbearable and if I really loved her I would cancel the holiday after my work and be home by Christmas. And you know, I do not want to cancel my holiday and am not even sure … well, about anything any more. This feels like the first time in my life I have really been on my own and not responsible for someone else, and I am liking it a lot. Is that so dreadful of me?'

'Nope. Is she your first?'

'You mean woman lover, partner?'

'Yeah.'

'No, the second. I was with someone for two years when I was doing post-graduate study at Leicester University, about 1981. She left me to get married and when I finished my studies I got the job in Middlesbrough. Mother wasn't well even then, so living close to Whitby seemed like a good idea. It was a shock when Father died first, '86 that was, he had a stroke and was gone, just like that.'

'No relationships in all that time, huh?'

Jane looked bashful. 'I guess I have never been adventurous in that regard. Actually I have never been adventurous, full stop. Now I am thirty-nine, and I want adventures, not a child. That is rather pathetic I suppose.'

'Not necessarily. What about brothers and sisters, did they help with your parents?'

'Not really. There is one of each: Ange lives in Liverpool with her husband and four children and Joshua teaches English in Japan with a Japanese wife he has never brought home. Everyone, including me, assumed that I would, you know, the unmarried daughter, take responsibility for our parents. And I never minded, not at the time, though I was a bit resentful that the little money mother had to leave was split evenly three ways. I suppose that was mean-spirited.'

'Hardly. Look, I don't think there's anything I can say, except it's obviously really hard and I'm glad it's not me.' Poppy was staring at the western hills. 'Hang on, I'll just say one thing; it sounds to me as though you have done a lot in your life to suit other people and maybe this is a chance to do what you want. That's it, no more from me, except that I'm pleased you told me what's going on, I really hate not knowing stuff, it gets me all in a tangle and I was beginning to get the idea there was something going on.'

The final angles of sunlight sent yellow and pink rays that bounced off the fast-moving cirrus clouds and stained the tops of fluffy cumulus.

'Shall I ring Rina – do you want to come to the party?' Poppy looked at Jane for the first time since she had joined her on the step. Jane shook her head.

'Thank you, but no, I am not at all in a party mood,' she managed a weak smile. 'I think I will sort out my notes, maybe check my email if that is all right, and have an early night. If I wake early I may walk up Maungawhau. Thank you, for listening, and for being kind. I'm not feeling so good about myself right now. And thank you for today, it was lovely, I really enjoyed it.' With a small squeeze of Poppy's arm, Jane jumped up and went inside.

Poppy watched the last few minutes light, marvelling at the back-lit clouds on the horizon, golden-rimmed as the sun slid away. She was looking forward to the party; many of her old friends would be there and she hadn't danced in ages. 'Have you been there all along?' She reached behind her to stroke Mrs Mudgely, who was rubbing against her back. 'What do you think of our visitor now, then? Is she in a bind, or isn't she? I guess it's for us to stay out of it, right?' Poppy supposed Mrs M's head was nodding in agreement. She jumped up, made and ate a sandwich, had a shower, dressed in black jeans and a blue t-shirt and knocked on Jane's door. 'I'm off. Plenty of food in the kitchen. See ya.'

'Goodbye, and thank you again for today,' Jane called out without opening the door. 'See you tomorrow.'

The party was noisy and crowded, with people surging in and out of rooms and spilling onto the front verandah and into the garden. For the first hour Poppy was in the thick of it, shouting catch-up con-versations and exchanging 'drop in some time' or 'give me a call' with a dozen or more women. When she noticed the back porch was empty, she went out and leant on the rail, taking deep breaths in the night air and searching among the patchy cloud for constellations she recognised.

'Hello, stranger, long time no see,' said a voice beside her.

'Leanne! Heavens, it must be twenty years, where have you been?'

'Living in cheaper places than Auckland, getting by on the benefit. What about you?'

'Teaching. And I bought a place in Mt Eden a few years ago. You knew Kate …?'

'Yeah. I cried for a week. You really cut me out there. And you know the Grafton Road house fell apart once you two left. We never got any decent flat-mates after that; in fact, I got ripped off by a couple and I ended up landed with back rent and phone bills. All that for four years of my life for the movement.'

'The movement …?'

'Yeah, the feminist movement, gay liberation, all that. You were never really into it, were you? Nor was Kate once she took up with you.'

Poppy couldn't take in what she was hearing. She stared at Leanne.

'The trouble with you middle-class sorts is you don't know what it is to struggle, really struggle. You never did get it, did you? There's my ride, gotta go or I'll have to walk to Henderson. See ya.'

She left Poppy stunned, her mouth open, her stomach churning. Two young women came out of the lighted kitchen, arms around each other, clearly wanting to be on their own. With a 'Hi' Poppy stepped past them and into the house, looking about. She spotted Martia at the far end of the living room and waved. Martia waved back, looked across the packed room and shrugged. Poppy pointed towards the front of the house, mouthing, 'Front garden, now, please!' She managed to gather up Eve on her way through the crush and when the three of them were out on the front lawn, sitting on one of the rugs scattered about, Poppy told them about her encounter with Leanne.

'Was I really like that, insensitive and ignorant and thoughtless and …'

Eve held up her hand. 'Whoa there. We all were a bit. We certainly didn't any of us understand the class thing, and I'm not sure I do even now. And at the same time Leanne has made rather a meal of being hard done by for a long time.'

'I didn't know. I didn't know anyone resented me like that, well not any other lesbian anyhow. And she seems to think I stole Kate off her ...' Poppy shook her head. 'And it's all so long ago now, it seems unreal. She just said all this stuff, like she's been wanting to for years, and walked off.'

'Forget it Pops.' Martia put an arm around her shoulder. 'Life is a big disappointment to Leanne, she expected to overthrow the patriarchy in a couple of years and – actually I don't know that many of us had thought about what would happen after the revolution.'

10

1991

It was a grey November Saturday in London and the petunias in the occasional window-boxes on Poppy's route to Brent Cross Station were bedraggled and browning. The spaces in front of the terraced houses – 'gardens' would not describe them – had mostly been paved for car parks. Papers and plastic swirled listlessly about in the light wind and she walked carefully, watching out for dog droppings on the footpath. The traffic roaring around and above her on the fly-over barely entered her consciousness these days. As she walked into the shelter of the station it began to drizzle. Two Moorgate trains went by before one that would take her to Tottenham Court Station where she could get the Central Line to Marble Arch. (She had learnt to avoid changing on the underground at Bank Station.) Even the cheerfulness she caught from the toddler in the pushchair waving and playing peek-a-boo faded when she noticed the shabbiness of both the pushchair and the mother's coat. When the mother shook the pushchair, saying, 'Don't annoy the lady, Timmy,' Poppy gave him a final wave and wink and subsided into gloom.

Katrina had persuaded her, almost a year ago, to come and stay with George in North Yorkshire for the summer – in New Zealand – holidays. Katrina had been resolved and Poppy had had no energy to argue after dragging herself through the nine months since Kate had died, refusing to leave the flat she and Kate had shared, refusing to have anyone come and share it with her even though the rent was punishing for one person. She had slept in their bed, cooked in their kitchen and gradually sorted through Kate's belongings, struggling at times to decide what was 'theirs' and therefore now hers and what had been Kate's and whether she should keep each one or offer it to someone else. There had been no will, so she was relieved when the Smiths made no claim on the 'estate'. Bob Smith had offered to deal with *Swift*, and Poppy had accepted gratefully and given it no further thought.

Her friends, she had been sure, had made a roster for ringing or dropping in at least once a day and she was touched by that; once she had decided she would go to George's she invited them all to lunch and gave each two small presents, one that was something that had been Kate's and one she had bought. Finding something especially for each of them had taken her hours of shopping which had been one distraction she could bear.

Belinda had come around once and gone through Kate's clothes with her, taking away a few bits of family jewellery and some photos of Kate as a child. They had cried together as they chose which childhood photos each would keep. Neither had made any contact with the other through the rest of that year, though Poppy had occasionally intended to, and occasionally felt guilty that she hadn't. 'There are two ends to a phone, dear,' had been Katrina's response when Poppy admitted her guilt at neglecting Kate's mother.

When she had arrived at Heathrow, George was there with his car. She could not remember the drive to Middlesbrough, and only hazily recalled anything at all about that Christmas. There had been a lot of people around, including Susanna's recently divorced daughter with her new partner and his teenage twin boys, and her older son and his wife and children. Poppy was grateful for their lack of interest in her and pleased to spend a lot of time in the kitchen, helping prepare meals or cleaning up after them. The weather had been freezing, cold and wet. Even the snow did not excite her, though she had liked walking on the Yorkshire Moors when she could borrow Susanna's car and drive herself there. She would walk for two or three hours in biting winds, snow flurries, rain or sleet, the bleak winter landscape more comforting than George's slightly oppressive concern and Susanna's meaningful looks and hand on her arm. Poppy felt mean-spirited every time she was resentful. She had thought she would return to Auckland in time for the new school year, but was overcome with lethargy whenever she tried to think about her life and work and where she would live now that her and Kate's flat was someone else's. George and Susanna urged her to stay on.

In mid-January she had been flipping through the *Yorkshire Times* when she saw an advertisement for relief teachers in London. By the end of that day she had arranged to start work in Camden the following Monday, five days away. The agency would provide her with a temporary place to stay.

It was easier being in London, even on her own. She got a bedsit in Brent Cross near the Northern Line station. The room was on the ground floor, facing north, at the back of the house of a large family who seemed to have endless dramas, but they didn't bother her, nor she them. She had her own toilet and basin and a tiny shower cubicle with a shower that dribbled rather than sprayed, but at least she didn't have to share it with anyone. The dark interior meant having the light on most of the time. A good electric heater, a jug and the smallest, cheapest microwave she could find to complement the hotplate in the 'kitchen' were all she had to buy. The rent was exorbitant by New Zealand standards but it included the power and no-one commented on what she used, so she kept warm and seldom thought about it. At first she thought she wouldn't bother to get the phone connected, but after a month changed her mind; the phone boxes that did work were hard to hear in for the traffic noise as often as not, and having her own phone meant people from home could ring her.

London she thought of as old. 'Even the footpaths are old,' she wrote in a letter to Martia, 'and it's grubby, and worn-looking, like very old jeans. There's not much earth, of the dirt kind, though more parks and trees than I remembered. You can grow tomatoes on a balcony in special plastic bags of soil that come with plants, fertiliser and instructions. Window-boxes, especially of petunias, are big in the better parts of town like Bloomsbury. There aren't many where I live.'

The first anniversary of Kate's death was hard. And because she died on Valentine's Day there was no avoiding a build-up to it, so she made herself unavailable for work on the Thursday and Friday and got the three trains to Middlesbrough, where George met her at the station late on Wednesday night. She spent most of Thursday on the Moors, grateful to be in a place that held no memories of Kate, where she could be alone, walking the paths, stopping when she wanted and sharing her lunch sandwiches with some birds she couldn't name. It was bitterly cold, with occasional patches of sun; she had learnt to dress for the weather. She nodded back at the few people she passed, and met George in the pub at Guisborough at four as arranged, knowing when he suggested it that he was looking after her still, making sure she got off the Moors before dark – in fact he had suggested they meet earlier – and felt touched rather than resentful now that she was not experiencing his concern several times a day.

They talked about Kate for a bit, Poppy letting the tears flow, George also wiping his eyes. Then Poppy asked George about his work at the museum, something he never talked of without prompting. 'Trichoptera will always be my first love,' he said, smiling at her vigorous nod, 'but I am increasingly interested in lepidoptera – you know.'

'Butterflies. Yes, indeed, I do know, how could I forget all those beautiful insect names you taught me? You've been at that museum a long time, it must be twenty years. Did you ever think of moving up, or on to somewhere else?'

He shook his head. 'Your mother was right, you know, I'm not ambitious. I like the things I know, and having one day much the same as another, and home comforts and taking a little bit of interest in local affairs. Susanna and I are well suited in that.' Poppy nodded. 'I'll retire in a couple of years,' George continued, 'and then I'll become one of the volunteers; I wouldn't know what to do with myself without my insects. I might even keep up with the lepidoptera when I retire; I've got rather fond of them and they're certainly more colourful than the humble caddis fly.' Poppy opened her mouth to speak and closed it again when he went on. 'I do miss you and Stefan and am sorry I don't really know Stefan's children. I especially miss you, dear Poppy. Stefan and I have a few rough edges with each other, but I miss you a great deal. I wish you'd stay a bit longer, you could get teaching work up here and ...'

Poppy was shaking her head. She put her hand on George's. 'That's not my life,' she said, 'though I will always want to visit, and I would love to come up in the summer and go on a bug-hunting trip with you, and Susanna of course.'

George was immediately enthusiastic. 'What a splendid idea! We'll go to the Lake District, there are some particularly beautiful tarns and streams that I need to get back to. Yes! We'll have a grand time!'

On the following Sunday's train journey back to London she had left *The Handmaid's Tale* largely unread, staring unseeing out the window for long periods, feeling the hard knot in her centre that was the remnant of what she had come to think of as her misery-fog. She had got used to it; it was so familiar it was almost comforting. She hugged herself and the knot inside. For a time she had felt it as a huge black ball, inside her instead of wrapped around her, less paralysing but heavy, bearing her down. Now it seemed more like a small, hard thing, a nut and bolt perhaps, holding itself in place inside her. She wanted it, welcomed it even. Without it she could forget Kate, could lose her all over again, she could not endure that, she would rather hold this hard thing inside her, and feel the loss and loneliness, because that way she still had something of Kate. Maybe she was starting to grow around it, the way a tree trunk grew around a nail

117

that had been hammered into its side, she could do that, she could grow around her hard thing, but it would always be there, inside her, and she would always have this part of herself that was Kate.

The man opposite was holding out a white, folded, ironed, hand-kerchief. Poppy shook her head and scrabbled in her bag for tissues. He smiled at her, a quick, slight smile and went back to his news-paper before he could have seen her smile back.

Once she returned from that trip she was able to focus on being in London, and as the weather got warmer, if not much less rainy, designed a day of every weekend around a *Michelin Pocket Guide to London* that Susanna had given her. She started with the 'must sees' and worked her way through them. The Tower of London was a surprise, it was so much more than a tower; she thought the ravens were majestic, especially when they spread their wings, and could see no doom in them at all. Disappointed in the British Museum with its serious scholars and literally, she thought, dry and dusty exhibits, she loved the Victoria and Albert. St Pauls, Westminster, the National Gallery, the Natural History Museum, Regents Park, Greenwich Village; she did them all.

Some became hers, places she returned to again and again, enjoy-ing them more as they became familiar. For wet days, there was the big room up the second flight of stairs from the main entrance to the National Gallery, holding on three sides large, buttoned, brown leather couches where she could sit for as long as she liked, reading, writing letters home, watching the people, or just sitting. Being among people, even feeling apart from them, was better than spending a whole day alone in her dark room. There came a time when a couple of the regular weekend guards would nod to her as they passed.

One wet Sunday, she noticed for the first time the mosaic floor at the top of the wide central steps up from the entrance. Apollo was in the centre (she knew it was Apollo only because his name was spelt out in the tiny tiles) surrounded by women in what she thought of as Greek draperies, looking outward in all directions, barely at him. She loved their names: Terpsichore, Melpomene, Polyhymnia, Urania, Calliope, Thalia, Clio, and thought for a moment that startled her – she had never wanted to have children – how nice it would be to have daughters with those names. The whole piece was bordered by a frieze of fruits. Then she realised there were more, more mosaics, on the next landing and on those to the left and right. Poppy walked around them all. To one side were separate images of people, each representing some activity: cricket, speed, hunting, contemplation, conversation, profane love, rest, swimming (with an obviously artificial sea-horse), dancing (an awkward rendition of a solo woman doing the Charleston) and football. A vine, also in mosaic, wound around, linking them all together into – what?

She wondered at the selection of subjects, at the laborious placing of pieces, each no bigger than a New Zealand one cent piece. Most people trod on them without noticing, as she had for several months. There was more: the other side, leading to the East Wing, had 'conversation' in the doorway, flanked by 'Christmas pudding' and – here Poppy laughed out loud, startling both herself and the people around her – 'mud pie'. And then, at the doorway to 'her' sofas another group, this time compassion, wonder, defiance (wasn't that Winston Churchill telling off something that looked like a griffen?), lucidity, leisure, curiosity. Plus, a pub – 'Rest and be Thankful' – and a tombstone. A guard came and tapped her on the shoulder. He pointed at a sign on the wall headed, 'The National Gallery Floor Mosaics (on the staircase landings)'. She smiled her thanks.

The mosaics, she discovered, had been laid between 1928 and 1952, were designed by one Boris Anrep and had been paid for by private donations. They represented life of the 'modern' age, she was further informed, and the present, this being the mid-1930s to 1950s, and each of the four sections had a title: Awakening the Muses (that was Apollo – oh, and Bacchus, she had missed him completely – and the accompanying women), Labours of Life, Pleasures of Life and Modern Virtues.

After this discovery and a further prompting from Katrina, who chided her in one of their telephone conversations about going to 'one of the most famous galleries in the world and hardly looking at the art works', Poppy worked her way around the galleries, two or three at a time. She liked the impressionists best.

On summer days when it was fine and not too cold, she made for Hyde Park, even though she had to change from the Northern to the Central Line to get there and the first time it took her three attempts to find the right exit from the underground station at Marble Arch. She seldom stopped at Speakers' Corner, mostly making her way to the banks of the Serpentine, where she had a favourite spot, sitting against a particular tree.

During a hot week in July some women at her current school were talking about a 'Ladies Pond' at Hampstead Heath and as the hot weather lasted until the weekend she investigated it. By the time she found the pond, via a back lane, she had covered quite a lot of the Heath. It was much less manicured than Hyde Park, with grass left to grow into unwieldy clumps and tangle around the legs of the park benches. There were dozens of these, many inscribed to a deceased loved one. At the top of Parliament Hill, the high point of the area, there was a bench every few metres, each angled for a particular view of London. The height and distance from the central city created a series of panoramas of old and new buildings. The old, stone and brick, low to the ground, multi-chimneyed, solid, brown, looking much more permanent than the newer, taller concrete and glass towers thrusting more aggressively upwards, the Post Office Tower the tallest of them all. Poppy found St Pauls and Big Ben with the help of the directory then sat on one of the benches, watching the waddling walk of the crows as they scavenged around recently-vacated seats, taking off in hard-working flight when people came near.

The Ladies Pond, she discovered, was aptly named. Only women were allowed, and they sat around on grassy slopes in various stages of undress but without full nudity – forbidden in the rules on a big wooden sign. Or swam. The pond was larger than Poppy had expected, and the water colder. She swam to the end and admired a blue heron flying off. There were a number of women on their own, like her, but most were in couples or groups, lying on towels, with hot or cold drinks, books, newspapers, magazines. Talking was definitely the favoured activity. Unconcerned birds walked around among the women. They looked like Pukeko, only smaller and less blue. Eventually Poppy found out they were moorhens. Two subsequent hot weekends encouraged her back to the pond before the end of summer.

While she went out from time to time for drinks or meals, occasionally a show, with people from the agency or the various schools she taught at, she never made real friends. Friends were people at home, the women who had carried her through those first awful weeks and kept phoning and coming round over the next months when she never phoned them, making her go out occasionally, doing things around the house that she hadn't noticed needed doing. These were her friends, people who had known her and Kate.

As the months went by, she stumbled across a Women's Learning Centre and did some volunteering there, and she went to the Silver Moon Bookshop regularly and some of their authors' readings. Occasionally someone she had met before would come up and greet her and she liked that, but she never initiated any further meetings. Unaware that she became the subject of gossip, with a reputation for being either 'a loner' or 'stand-offish' depending on who was making the comment, Poppy got to know central London well, but never felt anything but a temporary resident. She had a visa for two years, or was it three? It never seemed to be a problem, no-one had ever asked to see her passport, so she seldom thought about it.

Being a relief teacher presented its challenges. However, she could always leave them behind at the end of the day, and she was certainly never short of work; she began to turn down any jobs that required more than one change of line on the underground. The large pockets of poverty around London shocked her, but the malnourished, ill-dressed children she taught from time to time never felt like her responsibility. Nor did the aggressive or hostile behaviour she experienced in some classrooms; she learnt to deal with the immediate problem and forget it. It was the same with the polite, uniformed children in other areas; she taught as she was required, she thought competently, and they never made a real impression on her.

On August Bank Holiday she took the train to Windermere and met George for their bug-hunting expedition. Susanna had stayed home. It rained two of the three days, and the whole area was crowded with holidaymakers, but she loved the misty lakes and the damp walks, and didn't mind getting her feet wet wielding an insect net.

On a grey Saturday in mid-November two things happened: she realised she had been to all the places in the 'Exploring London' section of her *Michelin Pocket Guide* and she got a card from Katrina *… in a rush as usual, just to let you know, dear that I will be in Sydney for two weeks from tomorrow (8th), John and I are taking a holiday, he's been overdoing it …* It wasn't the message. It was the picture of a pohutakawa tree in full red bloom against a blue sky on the front of the card that made Poppy's eyes fill with tears of homesickness.

So she booked a flight home via Singapore on 9 December, wrote to Katrina asking if she could stay with her when she first got back, phoned George and told him, wrote a letter to all her friends, blessing whoever had invented photocopiers, told the agency she was leaving and gave notice to her landlady.

She would arrive home with enough money to keep herself for three months, longer if she stayed with Katrina who no doubt would refuse to take any rent. Getting a teaching job wouldn't be too hard, she thought; she could go anywhere around Auckland, or out of it for that matter, and take long-term relieving for a while if she had to. Where to live, and how – on her own? in a flat with others? – she couldn't answer; writing lists of pros and cons for as many options as she could think of didn't get her any further, so she decided she would have to wait and see, even though not having a definite plan made her anxious. She was not at all anxious about going home, though, she was ready, more than ready, for a New Zealand summer.

11

1999

The Sunday morning sun found a gap in Poppy's curtains and fell across her face, waking her. It was nine-thirty on the bedside clock; later than she usually slept, even at the weekend. She felt around the bed for Mrs Mudgely who was not there, which was even more unusual. It had been late when she came in, nearly two. After sitting on her own for a bit on Rina's front lawn, she had gone back inside, intending to find Rina and say her thank yous and goodbyes. She was still smarting from Leanne's comments and wanting to think for a bit, about her own life, and whether she had been – was – a 'good' feminist, or a feminist at all – she hadn't thought about that for ages – or even a good person. But Eve had pulled her into the midst of the dancing, and the music was her favourite, early Meg Christian and Holly Near, and suddenly it was very late.

She stretched, curled and stretched again, then swung her legs out of bed keeping the stretch going with her feet on the floor, reaching for the high ceiling. She'd get showered and dressed and go and see May-Yun she thought, and if Stefan wasn't … or maybe she should talk to them both at once, though what she could say without Chan feeling 'told on' she did not know.

Poppy knew she wanted to do something to help someone and

maybe she could help Chan. She smiled at herself. 'Not that I'm wanting to prove anything.' Mrs Mudgely walked in and jumped up on the bed. 'Hey, good morning,' Poppy scratched between her ears, 'have you been consorting with our guest?' There was no answer in the ensuing purr. 'Oh well, I'll just have to go and see for myself.' She pulled on a t-shirt and shorts.

'Good morning.' Jane was sitting at the table with coffee and the Sunday paper.

'Good morning to you,' Jane replied. She looked more cheerful than when Poppy had last seen her. She held up the paper, saying, 'This is an interesting country to be in at the moment. There's the America's Cup, a health scandal around cervical screening, and an election which might produce the first ever – anywhere I suppose – openly transgender member of parliament. How was the party?'

'The elections! Oh heavens they're only two weeks away and I've given them hardly any attention. The party? It was a party, you know lots of people, lots of invitations given and taken, I hope they don't all turn up today. I enjoyed myself, actually, apart from one blast from the past that set me back on my heels.'

'Oh, what was that?'

Poppy waved the question away, along with a twinge of guilt that she didn't read the paper more often. 'How about your evening?'

'Fine and very low key. I sent my first email report back to the museum and worked out my plan for the coming week, watched a bit of television, went to bed about eleven, and surprised myself by going straight to sleep. There's this insect, a cockroach, in advertisements about Y2K, about being prepared, having supplies of food and water. There hasn't been anything like that at home, should I be worrying about it, is there going to be a power blackout or computer meltdown or something?'

'Dunno. I can't take it too seriously myself. So much money is being spent on it, I guess I've decided to believe if there's a problem it'll be fixed pretty fast. You've been out and got the paper, then.'

'Yes. And I've been walking, I saw the sun rise from the top of Mung ...' she gestured helplessly towards the hill outside.

'Maungawhau.'

'Yes. It was wonderful. I got a big fright though, from some cows that came up behind me while I was sitting watching and listening to the birds. I went around the crater and down inside it and then to the shops. I've never stood in the bottom of a volcanic crater before, and never thought I would, under the eyes of half a dozen cows, anyway. This is a very beautiful place. Do you have a bird book, there were some I did not know?'

'Yep. There's one in there somewhere,' Poppy waved in the direction of a bookcase. 'Look, I'm going to pop over to my brother's. I don't want to be rude, but I'd rather you didn't come, I want to talk to them about my nephew and ...'

'That is not rude, and you have no obligation to take me places. I like it that you say things right out, and I do not have to guess what you really mean.' Jane was speaking slowly, with a slight, rueful smile. 'I have not thought what I will do, but time on my own is probably what I need. I think I might be having some kind of a mid-life crisis, everything seems to be changing – my work, my relationship and I'm having wild thoughts about ... well, wild thoughts. I may just stay in and seek some of Mrs Mudgely's wise counsel.'

'She's ...' Poppy stopped herself from saying 'mine' – 'good at that.'

When Poppy got to her brother's, the family was sitting around the table finishing an early lunch. They all greeted her warmly, made room for her at the table, and offered various items of food. She was pleased to see that Annie, who no longer lived at home, was there too.

'Yum.' She took bread, ham, pickles, olives. 'Why is lunch never this good at home? What have you guys all been up to?'

'I thought you might bring your English visitor to meet us,' said Stefan. 'George was positively smug in his last email about how well you two are apparently getting on.'

'Well, yes, Jane's easy to have around. I'll bring her over, another time. Or you could drop by my place.' Stefan never did that and Poppy knew he wouldn't and didn't let that stop her suggesting it.

She looked around the table. 'Well, what's the news?'

Ivan answered her. 'Annie was talking about flat-mates and how some of them have disgusting habits and Mum said she could always come back here and live and Dad said flatting was all part of growing up and then you came in. I don't think I'll ever go flatting, it's easier if you stay home, I reckon.'

Chan spoke, 'I'll ask you if you still think that in four years.'

'What do you mean, Chan?' asked his mother. He shrugged. 'Nothing, it doesn't matter.'

'We're all getting rather tired of your oblique comments,' said his father. 'Maybe you shouldn't say anything at all, unless you're prepared to say what you mean.' Chan looked at his plate, then at his father. 'Fine. I said it doesn't matter,' and he pushed his chair back, about to leave.

'Hey, Chan,' Poppy looked hard at her older nephew. 'Do you want some help?' She thought his face softened slightly as he looked at her and shrugged, so took a chance.

'When did you last listen, really listen, to what he has to say.' She was looking at her brother now. 'When did you last ask him what he thinks and feels about anything instead of telling him what he should be doing? When did you last tell him you love him, or appreciate anything he did or ...'

'That's enough!' Stefan banged his hand on the table and the dishes jumped. May-Yun had her hand across the table towards Chan. 'You have no right to come here and tell me how to treat my children,' Stefan continued. 'What do you know about family life, you with your, your ... lifestyle; you don't have any family responsibilities. This is my family and you can keep your nose out of ...'

Poppy was on her feet. She did not raise her voice, and spoke slowly. 'You are my family and I love you all. I will ignore your insults, Stefan, because Chan is unhappy and can't tell you about it because he knows you will disapprove and can't talk to his mother because he knows it wouldn't be fair to ask her not to tell you and you are just a silly, pompous ass.' Ivan snorted, Annie giggled and Chan looked fixedly down at the table. 'I'm sorry Chan,' Poppy went on, 'I've probably made everything worse,' and she subsided into her chair. She wanted to leave, hurt by what Stefan had said, but was determined to not give up on Chan.

'Will you tell us son?' May-Yun did not take her eyes off him. 'Will you tell us what is troubling you? Your father and I do want to know, and we will listen.' She turned and looked at Stefan, 'We will listen, won't we?'

He nodded, dismayed at his own outburst at Poppy and smarting at being called pompous. 'Yes, son,' he said finally, 'I would like to hear why you are unhappy, when you have every …' May-Yun raised her hand and he stopped.

Chan looked up and around the table. Annie smiled at him, and Ivan did a thumbs up. 'Go on, you can't make a bigger mess of it than I did,' said Poppy and grinned as best she could. May-Yun maintained her steady gaze.

'I'm the only one in this family that looks Chinese,' said Chan, quietly. 'Even you don't look as Chinese as I do, Mum.' He looked at her, then quickly away as her eyes filled with tears. 'I'll bet none of you have had people asking you how long you have been here and when did you immigrate and stuff like that; and then not believing you when you say you're a third generation kiwi.' Poppy saw he was struggling against tears himself. 'I feel like I've been made to be a Chinese person and I don't know anything about being Chinese. I don't want to study, I want to get a job and earn some money and go to China and find out about, I dunno, about my ancestors. Annie wants to make a film about Mum's family when they first came here, I want to find out about what it was – is – like in China, in southern China, the part they came from. I know it doesn't matter to the rest of you, but it does to me. That's all.' Chan was staring at his plate again.

May-Yun went and stood behind him, putting her arms around his shoulders and kissing the top of his head.

'Of course you must do this,' she said. 'There is very little information, I'm afraid, my grandparents brought my parents up to be New Zealanders and so it has been since. But we will find out what we can. I will help you. I have been very silly not to think about this sooner.'

Chan held her hands and looked up at his father; everyone was looking at Stefan. 'This is a complete surprise to me,' he said, 'I would never have guessed it, I thought – well, never mind what I thought, I couldn't have been more wrong.' He stood up. 'You must do what you must, son. We'll talk later about how to deal with your student loan.' He sat down again. 'Hell, am I really pompous?' Everyone except May-Yun nodded.

'Thanks, aunty.' Chan smiled at Poppy, whom he had never called 'aunty'. 'You've got balls.' The laughter relieved the tension. Poppy still had something to say to her brother, but it could wait.

Stefan looked at his watch. 'Ivan, we'll be late for your game if we don't leave right now. Do you want that ride back into town, Annie?'

'Can I come and watch?' Poppy asked Ivan. 'Sure thing,' he replied, 'I'm playing on the wing now, and in the junior A team. That's why it's an afternoon game. I'll get my gear.'

'May-Yun, we really do have to go.'

She looked at her husband. 'I think I will stay home and talk with Chan. I'll go and see if Ivan will mind.'

It took some minutes for Ivan, Annie, Stefan and Poppy to get to the car and get going. Poppy was pleased she would see Ivan play soccer and determined to make an opportunity to talk to her brother about her 'lifestyle'.

Ivan's team lost the game in spite of his goal. There was no doubt in Poppy's mind, after their side-line conversation, that Stefan really did believe that being a lesbian meant there were things 'missing' in her life and she would never get him to see that not only was there nothing missing, for her being lesbian was not only ordinary but also enriching. However, he had acknowledged her hurt at his comments about her not being part of the family and sort of apologised and she figured that was as good as it was going to get with him.

She refused May-Yun's invitation to stay for dinner. 'School tomorrow, planning to do.'

'Thank you.' May-Yun hugged her for longer than usual as she was leaving. 'I am ashamed that I did not know my own son.'

Chan walked out to the car with her. 'Do you know what I found out this afternoon?'

'No, tell me.'

'My Dad is an ordinary person, not big and fearsome. It's like we are both about the same size now, and I don't mean I'm about as tall as he is, and I've stopped feeling like the little kid.'

'Great. Send me a postcard from China.'

'Hey, slow down, it'll be a couple of years before I go, but it's cool to know I will.'

When Poppy got home Mrs Mudgely met her halfway up the steps. 'Well, hello, you haven't entirely abandoned me to our visitor then.' Poppy sat on the top step with the cat in her lap, stroking her in full sweeps from the top of her head to the tip of her tail. 'Who's a beautiful cat, then? Who's the best cat in the world?' Her murmurs were rewarded with loud purring.

Finally she went inside and found the dining table entirely covered by maps of New Zealand and travel brochures and Jane making notes. She made as though to clear them away when Poppy came in. 'No need to do that, I'd like to talk about holidays and travel, they'll be useful,' Poppy said. 'Have you been doing this all afternoon?'

'Not quite. I sat out in the sun for a while and finished the paper, had some lunch, checked my email and sent one home saying that I was not going to cut short my holiday here, having come this far, and so on.' Jane paused for a moment, then went on so quietly Poppy could only just hear her. 'It feels rather odd, I am so used to doing what other people want, especially if they are upset, and at the same time. I did make some suggestions for how Héloise could spend the holiday time, who she could stay with and who she could ask to stay. Then,' with a grin and a shrug, 'I deleted all that. I am too much in the habit of solving other people's problems, rather than letting them work out for themselves what they want to do. See, you are having an influence on me.'

'Oh dear,' there was contriteness in Poppy's voice. 'I've just been pushing things about with my brother's family and nearly had a real row with him. It worked out all right in the end, I think, but I've been reminded that my brother doesn't take my life seriously; because I've not got married and had children he doesn't quite see me as grown up. Katrina's the same. It's a bit depressing, actually. Still, I shouldn't complain, a lot of lesbians have it a lot worse with their families. But, dammit, it would be nice to be recognised by my relatives as a fully functioning responsible adult now and then, who has rather a lot of life experience and a fair dollop of good sense!'

'Well, I have been a complete coward with my family. I never told my parents at all about my, um, sexuality, and I have had so little to do with my brother and sister in the past fifteen years it has been irrelevant.'

'Don't they know about Héloise?'

'Well, yes and no. We exchange emails a couple of times a year about the state of the world in general and the weather and our holidays. I mention her now and then, as someone I share the house and go on holiday with, but I have never said she was my partner.'

'That seems more like a no than a yes to me, not that it's any of my business, and I've had my nose bitten once already today for sticking it in, so I'm backing off. Anyway I want to talk about something else,' and Poppy pulled out a chair and sat down. 'You look like you're making holiday plans. Have you got far with them?'

'Only to the point of knowing that I can't possibly do everything with the time and money I have.'

'Would you like a driver and companion for, well, part of your travels anyway? One with some local knowledge? I finish teaching on 17 December, and go back in late January for some training days and preparation, but other than that …'

'Oh, I would like that so much!' Jane face reddened slightly. 'I finish at Te Papa on the same day then am on holiday time until the end of January when I leave from Auckland, and I thought it would be sensible to go to the South Island from Wellington. Of course, you will want to spend Christmas and the New Year here with your friends and family so perhaps …'

'Yes, maybe, I'm not so sure. Christmas with the family and Don Smart-by-name I could certainly miss, I can do end of year stuff with Katrina and with Stefan and May-Yun and the kids earlier. The millennium New Year I haven't decided about. I had one little thought about taking myself off camping on the Coromandel, but I'm worried that people will pity me on my own and ask me to join in their parties, and I don't want that. If I party it will be with my friends'. Jane was nodding. 'I never know what to do when people are kind and I want to be on my own. I can't be on my own properly if people are feeling sorry for me and there are hardly any places now where you can camp rough; I'd be nervous about that by myself. This is a bit of a ramble, I know, but I'm so irritated by the millennium hype that I can't think what to do with it. Also, I don't want to horn in on all your New Zealand holiday, you might want some time on your own.'

'We could spend a lot of time looking out for each other and not deciding what we want to do ourselves.' Jane surprised herself with her statement. 'I would welcome your company and local knowledge on as much of my travels as you care to join me for.'

'Right. Great.' Now Poppy felt slightly nervous, and wasn't sure if that was because she might get herself into something she would regret or because she could see the looks on her friends' faces and knew only too well the conclusion they would leap to.

The two of them spent an hour with the maps and brochures, considering options in both islands but coming to no decisions, except that Poppy would stay in Auckland for some days after she finished at school and meet up with Jane in either Wellington or Picton on 23 or 24 December. Poppy made a note in her diary to book the ferry and they finished their planning session resolving to decide on a return date for the ferry in January by mid-week, on the assumption that ferry bookings would be heavy.

When Poppy got to school at seven-thirty on Monday morning, she found Tony sitting on the bench outside her classroom waiting for her. 'This had better not take long,' she told him, 'I've got a week's reading programme to set up for three groups and maths activities for today.' He followed her in to her classroom.

'It's Amelia,' he said. 'She's talking about leaving her husband.'

'And …?'

'And I don't want, well, um, to be responsible for, you know, breaking up her marriage and upsetting her kid and everything.'

'So you just wanted "a bit of fun" and some easy sex and now it's getting hard and you want out?'

'You don't have to be so blunt about it! But yeah, kind of.'

'Well, stop seeing her then. Tell her. Surely you don't need my advice to do that.'

'Uh, I thought you might …'

'Tony! You should know me better than that! Don't be such a coward, the only thing you can do is tell her, and tell her straight, as it were.'

'I can't deal with her when she cries Poppy, and I know she thinks highly of you – and so do I, of course – and I did think you could maybe suggest to her, you, know, that maybe she's taking things a bit too seriously.'

'Tony! You haven't been listening! No, and no, and no! You got yourself into this, you get yourself out of it! And stay away from married women if you can't handle the consequences. Now out! out! out! I've got work to do.'

'Okay, now that I feel like a complete heel …'

'You are.' Poppy put her hand on his arm. 'But I know it takes two to make this kind of mess, Tony, I don't think it's all your fault, I just think it's up to you to be honest with Amelia, no matter how she reacts. It's not fair to let her leave her marriage expecting you to be there if you're not going to be.'

When he had gone Poppy got on with her preparations. She saw Amelia arrive after eight-thirty and dash to her classroom, then the children started coming in and she had no chance to give attention to anything else. There were parents who wanted 'a word' as they dropped their child off, children who had something to tell or show her that couldn't wait until class began, and the general organised melée of the beginning of the week. Poppy loved it; she knew the children well and her systems and routines had been bedded in for months. Reading and maths materials were in place, in spite of Tony's interruption, and today she would introduce her last major science topic for the year, the characteristics and movements of the sun, its planets and their moons.

As soon as the children were settled on the outside benches with their lunches, just after twelve, Amelia appeared. 'I must talk to you!' she whispered to Poppy, 'It's really urgent.'

'I'm on playground duty at twelve-thirty, and I'm going to grab a cuppa and have a word with Moana about the old slide projector before that, so the earliest I can manage is after school. I'll be in my room until about half-past-four.' Poppy hoped her smile was friendly enough to take any sting out of her words.

'I could walk around the playground with you.'

'No.' Poppy was firm. 'I can't do playground duty and talk to you at the same time, come after school.'

'All right then. I suppose I'll get through the afternoon, somehow.'

'I do not feel guilty,' Poppy said to herself, catching a glimpse of a nodding Mrs Mudgely hovering over the doorway to her classroom, and turned her attention to the girl standing at her elbow. A few minutes later in the staffroom, waiting in line for hot water for her tea, she looked around at her colleagues, chatting in small groups, some of them about Tony and Amelia, for sure. Hugh was on his own, as usual, reading. When Moana came in most of them stopped talking and watched her. 'Waiting to see which group she will join,' thought Poppy, 'they are like children wanting the attention of teacher.' 'Stop that!' she told herself immediately.

The Principal in fact joined her, and suggested they go to her office to discuss the slide projector as she had some figures there. The slide projector was dealt with in a couple of minutes; Moana had found some money in the budget to buy a new one, and would talk to the whole staff about which model would best suit their purposes. As Poppy was about to leave she asked her to wait.

'What is it with Tony and Amelia?' she asked. 'I wouldn't ask you except their goings-on are affecting everyone and – in Amelia's case in particular – their teaching. I walked past her classroom on Friday afternoon and it was in an uproar and she was sitting at her desk staring into space.'

'I really don't want to talk to you about them, Moana, it seems under-hand.' The misery on Poppy's face brought a smile to Moana's.

'You're right, of course. I hate to pry into my teachers' private lives, but when it impacts on the school, I have to. Okay, I'll find out from them, starting with Tony, I think.'

Even without Amelia's company Poppy was distracted as she walked around the playground. All her life she had noticed when people were dishonest or dissembling, it had always made her anxious. The one time she had missed it was with her parents; she could still almost feel the shock of Stefan insisting that Katrina and George had been unhappy long before they had separated. She was beginning to feel like the conscience of the world, like a prissy Pollyanna, doing the right thing ad nauseum. On the other hand Leanne didn't seem to think she 'did the right thing'. And at the same time, she felt she was right, with her brother's family, with Jane, with Tony, and now with Moana; she didn't want to have said anything very different. Nor did she want to be a goody-good, like the girl in the television programme who was an angel or witch or something and made things better for everyone. She just wanted to get on with her life and …

'Hey miss,' a voice and a tug at her sleeve jolted her attention back to matters at hand. 'Justin's not sharing the ball.' By the time she had sorted out the dispute, her mind was firmly back in the world of the primary school lunchtime playground.

The last child was barely out the door at three o'clock when Amelia appeared. Poppy sighed and put down the atlas where she was marking a map of the planets with removable stickers. She considered telling Amelia about her success introducing the science topic with the class out in the playground, a child in the centre holding a large cut-out of the sun, children with cut-outs of planets and moons in more or less relative size to each other, if not to the sun, shepherded into position and moving, planets around the sun, moon around the planets, and all with their own spin. Crude science perhaps, but she was thrilled at how many had got the overall idea of the whole picture. One look at Amelia's face, however, and she abandoned any idea of talking about anything except her and Tony. Amelia sat on one of the children's desks, near to Poppy's table. Her face was flushed, her eyes bright.

'I'm going to leave Ian,' she announced with a dramatic flourish of both arms. 'He has accused me of lying and deceit, and been so awful. I am going to tell him tonight that I am in love with Tony and I'm taking my baby and leaving.'

'Hardly a baby,' thought Poppy, and said, 'What does Tony say about this?'

'Oh Poppy, you could try and be a little excited for me. He says, I don't know what he says, but we are so good together, and the sex is so good and we laugh so much.'

'Has he told you he loves you?'

'Of course – well, not in those words you know, but we women can tell, can't we?' Poppy glanced around the room, expecting to see Mrs

Mudgely shaking with laughter. Yes, there she was, by the top of the door on the inside of the spot she had been in at lunchtime, shaking her head in despair more than laughing.

'Have you told Tony you are planning to leave Ian?'

'Yes, but we were … you know, we got distracted. I thought you would be pleased for me, pleased that I was happy.' She didn't look happy to Poppy, rather what Katrina would have called 'over-excited' when Poppy was a child.

Poppy could not think what to say. She didn't want to repeat what Tony had said to her that morning, she didn't want to repeat what Moana had said at lunchtime and she couldn't pretend to be pleased. What she wanted to do was shake some sense into Amelia, but instead she took her arm and walked her towards the door saying, 'Come with me.'

'Where are we going? What are you doing?' Amelia was pulling against Poppy's grip but following her nonetheless. It was soon apparent that they were heading for Tony's classroom. 'Please be there, Tony,' Poppy was saying to herself, 'Please be there, damn you.' He was there, and so was Moana, they were talking, both with their backs to the door so they did not see Amelia and Poppy until they were well into the room. 'Omigod,' thought Poppy, 'get me out of this soap opera.' She pulled Amelia right up to Tony, dropped her arm and took hold of Moana's. 'Oh good', she said, 'I need to talk to you urgently about … about … the slide projector.' And she marched the startled Moana out of the classroom.

As soon as they were around the corner of the building Poppy let go Moana's arm and put her hand over her mouth. 'Sorry I bundled you out like that,' she began.

'Don't be. I had just asked Tony if he was interested in a year's secondment to the College of Education next year. I hope he takes it.'

The two women looked at each other, spluttered, and began to laugh, taking gulping breaths to stop themselves when they became aware of two other teachers approaching. Moana looked at her watch and said, when she got her breath, 'The Empire, four-thirty, drinks on me.' At Poppy's nod she strode purposefully off towards her office. Poppy went back to her classroom determined to concentrate on her work rather than speculate on what Tony and Amelia might be saying to each other.

When she arrived at the local pub, Moana was already there. Neither of them mentioned Amelia or Tony. After some desultory chat about the coming holidays they talked about teaching and careers and Moana enquired about Poppy's long-term plans. Poppy found herself explaining yet again how she was happy as a classroom teacher and had no ambition to become a principal or even a senior teacher, what she liked was working in a classroom with 'her' children for a year, taking part in their development and working reasonable hours, unlike Moana, who nodded all the way through Poppy's speech.

'My career cost me my marriage,' she commented at the end, 'partly because I didn't want to interrupt it to have children. Now I have a "friend",' she went on, 'an older man with a grown-up family who has his own place. We go out together, have holidays, go to one of his daughters' for Christmas, that kind of thing. With him being older, there's not as much sex as I would like perhaps, but sex isn't everything – as I just told Tony! – and Robin suits me, and I think I suit him. What about you?'

'I don't have a partner at all at the moment and that suits me.' Poppy hesitated, then ploughed on. 'The love of my life, Kate, died suddenly in an accident nearly ten years ago.'

'That must have been very hard. I'm sorry.'

'Yes, it was the hardest thing ... there has been someone – a woman – since, but that didn't work out.'

'I am thankful to be living now and not fifty years ago, when my mother was widowed with four children and then criticised for going out to work,' said Moana, 'and I guess you are too, for different reasons,' she was gathering her things as she spoke. 'I must be off.

Thank you for coming.' She stood, hesitated, and turned back to Poppy, 'I am very glad to have you on my staff,' she said, gave a little wave, and was gone.

'How different,' thought Poppy, 'how different from 1985, when I was terrified I would lose my job because I signed a newspaper advertisement.'

Over the next few weeks, Poppy avoided the staffroom as much as she could, unwilling to take part in the gossip about Amelia and Tony. She avoided the two of them as well, grateful that Amelia had found other women on the staff who were no doubt more sympathetic to her plight and no longer sought her out.

Jane was out a lot with various people from the museum and spent one weekend with Peter Voss and his family at a show-jumping event at Drury. In the mornings when Poppy was rushing to beat the traffic, Jane was usually up with coffee made, having already walked to the dairy for the paper.

'I could get it delivered,' Poppy offered on the Saturday morning of election day, 'then maybe I would read it more.' But Jane insisted she liked the walk and was on greetings terms with the family in the dairy; she was often their first customer when they opened. Curious about the polling booths, Jane walked to the local school when Poppy went to vote, then they each went about their own activities, joining up again to watch the results come in on television. When it became clear that Georgina Beyer – the transgender candidate – had won in her electorate they exchanged high fives, after Poppy had taught Jane how. Poppy didn't stay up for the speeches.

On Sunday morning Jane made breakfast, as had become her habit. Over pancakes, fresh fruit, cream and, of course coffee, they read and swapped sections of the paper. 'More coffee?' Jane held up the empty pot.

'Sure, why not, here I'll make it, I've read enough newspaper for one Sunday.' Jane grinned at her. 'I don't see that that's funny.' Poppy was slightly defensive. 'Not funny, exactly,' said Jane, 'I was just wondering how you would get on with the *Independent on Sunday*, or the *Guardian*.'

'I have lived in England, you know. And the Sunday papers were easy enough to deal with. You just buy one and dump the two-thirds of it you don't want to read in the first bin you see.' Poppy raised her voice as she went into the kitchen. 'And some Sundays, you can have time off and not buy one at all.'

'That's one of the things I am really enjoying here,' Jane was leaning on the doorway to the kitchen, 'the way people don't take things too seriously, instead of being weighed down by them, you find a solution.'

Poppy's raised her eyebrows. 'I don't understand.'

'Take you and the Sunday paper, you find it dauntingly big so you throw away most of it and just keep the bit you want to deal with, instead of keeping it all and complaining about how heavy it is to carry and how it takes up your whole Sunday reading it, which is what English people do.'

When she had poured the hot water on the fresh coffee grounds, and replaced the plunger, Poppy headed back to the diningroom table. 'You know I've been to North Yorkshire and around there, with George living in Middlesbrough, but only for a few weeks at a time, what's it like when you live there?'

Jane shrugged. 'Depends on where you live and how much money you have, the same as anywhere. I love the coast, around Whitby, where I grew up, but even that is changing as the best areas get more and more upmarket and expensive. Billingham, where Héloise and I live, is the centre of Britain's petrochemical industry, did you know that?'

12

1999

The mountain-tops were under cloud as Poppy drove along the Desert Road. It was two days before Christmas and she was glad to be out of Auckland. She had seen all her family, and seen or rung her close friends except for Bessie and Alexa who were on holiday with Alexa's parents on the Gold Coast. Mrs Mudgely was at Moggy Manor in Drury. MM was run by two extremely brisk and efficient women in their sixties, who remembered Mrs M from one 'visit' to the next. Nevertheless Poppy felt guilty leaving her for four and a half weeks and wished she had found someone to stay in her house while she was away.

Tiring of the slow-moving camper van in front of her, and unsure how far it was to a passing lane, she pulled into a rest area, got out of the car and stretched, admiring the tawny browns and pinks of the tussock stretching away on both sides of the road and the strong, dark presence of Ruapehu in the grey day, even though only the lower half of the mountain was visible. The traffic roared past; it was going to be a slow haul to Wellington where she was meeting Jane at the front of the ferry building at eight-thirty p.m.; the only ferry booking she had been able to get was the ten p.m. crossing.

She had left early and it wasn't yet midday, but with the traffic this heavy she could count on another five hours' driving to Wellington, so with several stops, essential to any long trip, she had about the right amount of time. The air on the plateau was cold and the speeding traffic close, so she didn't linger.

Poppy resigned herself to slow driving to the singing of Ferron and Suede, pleased she had remembered to bring tapes. Roadside cafés and tearooms were doing a booming trade. Taihape was the place she had selected for her next break, which she cut short when she saw the queues. It was nearly one-thirty and she was hungry so she bought a packet of sandwiches at a dairy, a slightly over-ripe banana, and an apple that had probably been parted from its tree too long ago, and drove on to the next rest area. Two families and an elderly couple were there ahead of her and had taken up all the picnic tables, so she sat on her swimming towel on the grass. Having worked out that even at her enforced slow pace she could be in Wellington by five o'clock – therefore she had three hours to spare – she washed the unappetising lunch down with the cold water she always carried and lay down on the towel.

Clouds still covered the sun but the air was fresh rather than cold; she breathed it in deeply and allowed herself to relax. The end of the school year had had its usual rushes and dramas, plus the ongoing saga of Amelia, who was back to mending her marriage to Ian; Tony had become the predator who played on her vulnerability because her marriage had hit a rocky patch … Poppy could barely listen to her rationalisations and self-justifications by the end of term. As for Tony, the only way apparently he could extricate himself was to blame Amelia and he had accused her of entrapping him, of giving him the impression that all she wanted was a bit of a fling, 'and what's the harm in that?'. At least the rest of the staff were, on the whole, thoroughly fed up with both of them, too. And that was quite enough attention to be giving to them, Poppy resolved; not another thought on that subject until school went back.

She was concerned about Martia though, who had seemed

extraordinarily tired and in unusually low spirits when she came around to dinner two days before. 'Nothing to worry about,' she had brushed aside Poppy's concern, 'just my usual Christmas blahs, I've got caught up in the family thing again and I do hate it. Barb and I are off to the Coromandel for a few days in the new year, that'll set me right.'

The mysterious Barb and Martia had become lovers three years earlier; she'd moved into Martia's house, but they hardly ever went anywhere together and while Poppy saw Martia every two or three weeks she had only met Barb half a dozen times. 'We don't like the couples stuff, we get on fine together in bed and around the house and on holiday and we have different work and friends and they don't overlap much. End of story.' And that was all Poppy could ever get Martia to say about her relationship, which rather hurt her feelings because they were best friends, weren't they?

Two more cars turned into the rest area; time to move on. Returning her towel to the boot of the car, Poppy looked over its contents. There was her tent, the one she and Kate had used, and she had used on her own since; it was just big enough for two, roomy for one, igloo-style, quick and easy to put up. Alongside it lay the almost identical tent she had borrowed from Stefan, the one her nephews slept in when the family went camping – this year they were going to May-Yun's brother's in the Waikato for a farm holiday and Chan was going too, on a promise of his mother and uncle pooling what they knew about the family's origins. They knew their grandfather had emigrated from Toishan province in Southern China in about 1915 and brought his wife into the country before legislation had restricted the immigration of family members.

Poppy had found planning this holiday easier once it had become clear that they would not be living in the intimacy of a shared tent. Stefan had offered them their big family one with the solid aluminium frame, but they had quickly agreed on the two smaller tents, overtly, at least, for their ease and speed of assembly.

Beside the tents, in the boot were a two-burner gas cooker with full bottle, two folding canvas-seated stools, a small folding table (that May-Yun insisted they should take) a solar shower, a large and a small chilly bin, and a first-aid kit including lots of suntan lotion and insect repellent. There were also sleeping bags, self-inflating mattresses, pillows, a box of cooking and eating utensils, two large water bottles – they would certainly not be doing it rough, but would be self-sufficient enough to camp in places without facilities for a few days if they wished. The bucket with a lid was squeezed in one corner, a supply of non-perishable food in the other.

Back on the road to Bulls, with Sweet Honey in the Rock as loud as her car stereo would allow Poppy enjoyed the dramatic white cliffs along the far river bank, and the beauty of the poplars, now in their full summer green. HospitaBull in Bulls, between CollectaBulls and FixaBull (hardware!) had good coffee, she discovered, more than ready for it at three in the afternoon. It was noticeably warmer now she was down off the plateau and the cloud was broken, allowing patches of sunlight through. She probably had time for a swim, she thought, so when she got back to the car she studied the map for where the road ran closest to the sea. Paekakariki looked like her best chance and she became aware of the first glimmer of anticipated pleasure, singing along to Heather Bishop. 'Yes,' she thought, 'I'm on holiday, a real holiday, far from home, with good company ahead.'

Jane was good company. By the time she left for Wellington, Poppy was enjoying her being in the house. Jane had met May-Yun and Stefan and Katrina and most of Poppy's friends, and everyone told Poppy how lovely she was. Poppy would agree with them and refuse to discuss the 'implications' that her friends in particular were excessively curious about. She hadn't herself noticed that her friends' curiosity intensified her own tendency to keep a distance between herself and Jane; they had reached an unspoken agreement that there would be no more intimate conversations about their pasts or presents. If asked, either of them might have said that there had not been the opportunity.

The hour to Paraparaumu passed quickly, and soon after that Poppy began looking out for the Paekakariki turn-off. She ignored the invitation to 'Fly by Wire' and turned across the railway lines into the village. Driving past the pub on the corner and a small cluster of shops, she couldn't see the sea, but figured it to be over the incline straight ahead, and so it was. Right there, the wide, open sea. Kapiti Island to the north, and the road separated from the beach by a breakwater. She drove along slowly, inordinately pleased with whatever planner had placed the road so there were no houses between it and the beach; houses lined the other side, and clambered up the hillside beyond. Where to stop? A bit further down maybe, where there were some people swimming. Where to change? Under her beach towel if necessary; she couldn't see any changing sheds.

The woman walking along the footpath, a large cloth bag under one arm, the other hand on her head holding a straw sun-hat in the wind, looked familiar. The woman started, waved, and ran towards the car. Poppy pulled over and stopped, laughing and incredulous.

'What the ...'

'I don't believe it.' Jane was laughing too. 'This is impossible! I came out here yesterday. Miranda at Te Papa lives here with her partner and their daughter, I think I told you in an email, and they invited me out. I was on my way to the five o'clock train – they offered me a ride but I wanted to walk ... How come you ...?'

'I decided I had plenty of time for a swim. Anyway, get in before a car comes, and hello.'

'Hello to you too.' Jane was still shaking her head. 'I do not believe this country, everyone knows everyone else, well nearly, and well, here you are and our arrangement to meet was not until eight o'clock and somewhere else.'

'Yeah. Small. Have you had a swim today?'

'Two, but I could stand another. We could go and change at Miranda and Jane's – and that made for some confusions, her having the same name as me, especially for little Jemma.'

'I'd rather not go to their house and get involved in socialising and cups of whatever. I could teach you my foolproof technique for changing on the beach.' Poppy did not want to deal with meeting the two women. Jane – the other Jane – had had an affair with Rose just before Poppy and Rose got together, and Poppy did not know whether Miranda knew about that or not. She didn't explain, just drove a little further down the road until she found a place where she could pull off and park. They clambered down the rocks that made up the breakwater to the sand and Poppy demonstrated how she held a towel, undressed, and put her togs on while retaining some modesty. 'The trick,' she explained, 'is to do it quickly and without a fuss and then even if you do display some naked body chances are no-one will notice.'

'"Togs", is a very New Zealand word,' commented Jane. 'I like it. My English shyness or prudery or whatever it is has certainly been shaken up in the last few days. Miranda comes in from the sea, strips by the clothesline, hoses off the sand, and wanders inside into the shower stark naked. I don't think I could do that.'

They gasped at the coldness of the water at first. The sea was too boisterous for serious swimming, but Poppy managed a few strokes, then body-surfed on the bigger waves. Jane refused to change back into her clothes on the beach, asking Poppy to stop at the public toilets near the shops for her. When she came out she was looking pleased with herself.

'I have an idea,' she said, putting her bag on the back seat and climbing into the front one. 'We have plenty of time and the place down the road called The Fisherman's Table is open right through lunch to supper. I can shout you an early meal there, then you drive me to the Backpackers for my bags and we can be at the ferry in plenty of time. What do you think?'

'Fine,' answered Poppy, 'but there is no need for you …'

'You have saved me a taxi fare to the ferry, and I want to thank you for coming with me. My time in Wellington has been so much easier with the contacts you gave me, and I have had such amazing experiences like driving over the hills to Martinborough and lunch in a vineyard, right among the vines, it was wonderful, and dinner out in all sorts of places, and at people's homes. There are some astonishing houses on the hillsides in this city and the museum is really state of the art, world class and I learned so much there, oh, and the coast out from Martinborough – I still struggle with the Maori place names – Wai …'

'The Wairarapa Coast?'

'Yes, that sounds right. There is some wild coastline around Cornwall, but nothing like that, tho' driving around Moa point reminded me of some parts of Cornwall. Even walking every morning is a delight, from my digs in Thorndon to Te Papa – as long as the wind was not tooooo cold, and I only got really rained on once – and back again, except I didn't do that often because I got so many invitations and I was actually rather pleased to not spend too many evenings in. The women in the flat were very nice, and it was so close I could walk to most places but they are very young and their lives are so different, I couldn't tell who was with whom, and it didn't seem to matter to them and they were constantly rushing in and out again and their music was loud and …' She came to a sudden stop. 'I must sound like a real old fuddy duddy. Anyway, once I had finished at the museum, I moved myself to the Backpackers. Oh, here we are.'

'Yep', said Poppy, 'I pulled into the car park several minutes ago.' Jane blushed.

'Oh dear, I did go on rather. Sorry.'

'I'm glad you're having a good time.'

'Thank you. And thank you again for, well, everything.' Jane spilled things out of her tidily packed bag as she looked for her wallet and shoved them back in any old how.

Because they were early, there was a free table on the balcony overlooking the sea, provided they were willing to vacate it for an eight o'clock booking. The restaurant filled fast, with groups of what Poppy assumed were work colleagues for their end-of-year party. She insisted that they order from the special menu – $13.95 and as many trips as you like to the salad bar. Both had fish and a glass of white wine and they were ready to leave by seven. Two shags, 'cormorants to me,' Jane explained, were drying their wings on rocks by the road to Pukerua Bay.

'I'm sure they are smaller than the cormorants on the Cornwall Coast.' Jane was turning in her seat to keep them in view. 'But it might be that you don't see them so close here.'

The traffic was heavy in both directions on the winding, narrow road. 'Pre-Christmas madness,' said Poppy, 'it's like a sickness that takes over the country for a week. I hate it.'

'It certainly is different in England,' replied Jane, 'and not just the weather. It gets dark so early at home in December and is so cold and miserable that the lights and the singing are quite cheering, even if you ignore the Christian parts of it.'

'Do you? Ignore the Christian bits, that is.'

'On the whole, at least since my parents died. Héloise's response to the whole thing is "bah, humbug", she's all for going back to pagan rituals.' Jane paused, wishing she had not thought of her partner. 'Anyway, I went through the motions while my parents were alive, mostly to keep them happy. I grew up Anglican, but drifted once I got to university and it stopped making sense.'

'Christmas here is all mixed up with summer holidays and the end of the year, and it's a bad combination, I reckon. It's light until after nine, for heaven's sake, and too damned hot for turkey and Christmas pudding, though plenty of people don't do that any more.'

There was no empty parking space at the backpackers' opposite the railway station. 'I have already checked out, my luggage is being held at the desk,' said Jane, 'you double park while I run in and get it.'

An image of a smiling, nodding Mrs Mudgely appeared for a moment on the bonnet of the car. 'Right on, Mrs M,' said Poppy, 'right on.' She echoed the smile and turned to open the back door for Jane's backpack to go on the seat. 'Boot's full of camping gear. I've got a plan for the next twenty-four hours. Subject to approval of course. Want to hear it?' Jane was back in the front passenger seat. 'Yes, of course.'

'Hang on a minute though, I can't stay here, I'm blocking traffic. I'll need to concentrate for a minute.' Driving in Wellington was new to Poppy, she didn't know the turning lanes and the traffic was heavy, so there was no conversation for nearly fifteen minutes, and then there was a sign to the inter-island ferry, so she followed that and they ended up near the front of the vehicle queue half an hour early.

'Phew.' Poppy let out a sigh of relief. 'I guess we could go over to the terminal and get a coffee, or we could stay here. Whatever, I'll finally tell you my idea for a plan. I hope my driving wasn't too scary, I don't know this city.'

'Your driving is very competent. And I would just as soon stay here and hear your plan and watch all this.' Jane gestured around her. 'But if you want a coffee …'

'Tell you what. You stay here, and I'll go over and get some take-away coffee. You might need these,' and Poppy handed over the tickets for the ferry, one for the car and one for each of them. She smiled, remembering the struggle she had had to pay for half the car ticket. They had agreed that as they were using Poppy's car Jane would pay for all the petrol they used on the trip. 'Just as well I filled up at Levin,' Poppy thought.

When she came back with the coffees, Jane was standing outside the car, looking over the harbour with her binoculars. 'Terns, I think, they're a bit far away to be certain. Have a look.' She swapped the binoculars for one of the coffees. It took Poppy a while to get the birds in focus. 'They look pretty much like seagulls to me, but then I'm ignorant about birds.'

'I love their simplicity and their beauty; sea-birds in particular. That's why I did my fieldwork on them. As I have told you already.

Oh my, it is good to be here, doing this! Tell me about your plan.'

'Oh, yes. Well, the ferry gets in to Picton at about one a.m. There's a motel there that has a late arrival/late checkout system, especially for ferry passengers I guess, so we could crash there and drive on to Nelson whenever we want tomorrow. And we will have slept and it'll be daylight so we could go via the shorter but slower and very windy – as in lots of corners – route that will give us some views of the Marlborough Sounds. Unless, of course, you want to see Blenheim.'

'Sounds rather than town seems good to me.' Jane laughed at her own rhyming. 'And I had wondered what we would do when we arrived. Which reminds me, you have done most of the bookings and organising so far, is that all right with you?'

'Sure, it's more efficient with local knowledge, and I don't mind a bit.'

'It's very nice to not be responsible for absolutely everything so that if anything goes wrong it's bound to be your fault.'

'I don't know what you are talking about.' Poppy was guessing an oblique reference to Héloise but did not want to collude in a month of allusions and indirectness.

Jane gave a small, embarrassed laugh. 'Of course you don't, that was a silly thing to say. What I meant is that I seem to have always been the person who makes holiday arrangements – or any sort of arrangements, in fact – with my parents, and with Héloise. And while I never minded, really, I have noticed that any problems, or mix-ups were then my fault. If you never arrange anything, I suppose it is never your fault if it goes wrong.' She shrugged.

'I guess you're right.' Poppy did not want to pursue this conversation. Ever since they met by chance she had sensed a change in Jane, a combination of her being both more at ease and more tense was the only way she could describe it to herself. She tried asking Mrs Mudgely for an opinion but there was no response, so she busied herself with maps and then the day's paper.

After a moment Jane took the field guide to New Zealand birds and her binoculars and leant on the car, scanning the wharf and the harbour and consulting the book. A man came by and collected their tickets, telling them that the ferry was on time and boarding would be in about fifteen minutes. The number of men wearing reflective yellow vests and their level of activity increased markedly over the next few minutes and Jane returned to the car without speaking.

Driving up and around the curving on-ramp Poppy remembered once having to back a van up that ramp, one of the last few vehicles to board. She had no idea when or in what circumstances she would have been driving a van onto the ferry but her memory of the experience was strong.

Without discussion they both took parkas, headed straight for the top observation deck, and sat at the front. There were a few clouds in the nearly-black sky and a light, cool wind. Poppy was hoping for some moonlight as they went through the Marlborough Sounds; she recognised a familiar wish, with any overseas visitors, to show off her home country at its best.

'Do you get sea sick?' Poppy had not thought to ask earlier.

'Only once, in the Shetlands, just after a storm.'

'Good, there's often a swell in Cook Strait. I don't think I get sea sick, but I'm nervous of the sea and haven't ever been on it when the weather was rough. Kate loved it.'

Jane put her hand on Poppy's arm, briefly. The ferry started moving. Jane said, 'I would like to tell you about my communications with Héloise over the past few weeks, since I left Auckland. Do you want to hear?'

'Sure.' Poppy gazed around the harbour at the lights, orange lines tracing the roads up and down the hills, and disappearing suddenly behind them, and yellow spots in thousands of windows where people were not on their way to anywhere. The lights danced in reflections on the ruffled harbour water. Neither woman looked at the other while Jane spoke.

'It wasn't easy to get email access at Te Papa or at the flat in

Thorndon so it was two days before I got that sorted out – I discovered the Wellington Public Library, actually, and it opens until nine so I could stop on my way home, when I was going home, that is. Anyway, communication was rather fraught. Héloise didn't understand that I would maybe not get her messages for twenty-four hours or even more. It feels as though we are suddenly in completely different worlds, and I don't just mean with me being here in New Zealand and her being in England, we seem to have gotten more and more out of kilter with each other since I came away. She wants me to make decisions about house decorating and new appliances and I don't even want to think about them, all that seems so unreal to me at the moment. So I have asked her to wait until I get back to make any decisions or purchases and she was cross and said did I want her to put her whole life on hold while I was away.' Jane paused and sighed, and looked at Poppy, who nodded, so she continued.

'Then, about two weeks ago she mentioned that she had met these two gay men, they live in Guisborough near the Moors and have plenty of money apparently and are interested in having children. That was all she said, so when I rang her at the weekend I asked and she avoided going into it but clearly she had talked with them about the possibilities of fathering and parenting, so I said again that she must not assume anything and she got upset and rang off. I was probably supposed to ring back but I stopped myself and our communications since then have been stiff and superficial. I find it really hard not to be conciliatory but I just cannot let myself in for twenty years of child-rearing. Yet if she wants to have a child, I cannot – do not want to – stop her. We seem to have come up against something where it is impossible for us both have what we want, just when I am trying to stop doing what everyone else wants instead of following my own way.' Jane stopped as her voice developed a wobble.

'Hard stuff, that, the hardest of all, wanting different things.' Poppy was brisk. She wanted to hug the other woman, but didn't – a holiday was one thing, anything more was out of the question while she was so entangled. They fell silent. A voice came over the ship's intercom warning that they were just about to enter Cook Strait and all passengers on the outside decks were asked to move to one of the inside lounges.

'Probably want us to buy food and drinks,' muttered Poppy, 'but we'd better go. I think there's supposed to be less roll lower in the ship so I'm going to head downstairs and read my novel and try not to imagine being sucked into the ocean depths.' When they had found a spot, Jane got the latest *Listener* out of her backpack but clearly could not settle to reading it. Poppy focused on her book. Maybe this had been a bad idea, she thought, but as long as she took care not to get embroiled in Jane's domestic concerns – she thought 'disasters' first and made herself change it – it should be all right.

Less than twenty-four hours later, at seven p.m. on Christmas Eve, they were setting up camp in Pohara, Golden Bay. The camping ground was nearly full, but they had a good spot with morning shade. 'Very important if you don't want to wake sweating in your tent at six a.m.,' was Poppy's opinion, so they chose this space over one that was slightly closer to the beach. Many of the campers were families, with children of all ages swarming on foot, on bikes, with balls and bats, swimming togs and towels.

'Scarborough was never like this,' said Jane. 'There is nothing here but sand and sea, grass and trees. No B & Bs, no shops – that store does not qualify as a shop – no entertainment arcades, no pier, what a wonderful place for children.' She laughed. 'Hark at me! What a wonderful place for anyone!'

There had been crowds of holiday-makers in Nelson and Poppy had had a couple of anxious hours wondering whether she had been foolish not to book ahead. They took advantage of the supermarket to do enough food shopping to last them several days, including Poppy's obligatory smoked chicken. 'I always have smoked chicken on the first night of a camping holiday.' She was adamant, even though they had to settle for a frozen one. 'It's all turkeys and capons and hams today,' commented the helpful assistant who had found it for them.

They drove on around the bay, and once they got to Motueka decided to push on over the hill to Takaka and Golden Bay. Poppy was gratified by Jane's ecstatic response to it all. 'This country is impossible!' Jane had exclaimed at one point. 'Every place demands that you stay a week and explore and I could get drunk on the scenery.' She had rung home from the motel before they left. Poppy had gone for a walk around Picton to give her privacy. When she returned Jane was quiet, and ready to leave.

'Okay?' asked Poppy.

Jane nodded. 'More or less. I told her I might not be in touch for a few days and she was not pleased but she did wish me Merry Christmas. And you. And for the first time said she wished she were here, with me. Anyway, tell me about these Sounds we are going to drive through.'

'Can't, I'm afraid, I've never done it before. By all reports the road is as winding as they get and the scenery stunning. If that rain doesn't eventuate.' There were some showers, but they got glimpses of the islands and bays of the sounds, and a sense of mystery and strangeness driving through the hills into Nelson with a light drizzle falling. Now it was cloudy but dry.

There wasn't much left of the smoked chicken after they finally got to eat it, with lettuce and tomato and fresh bread. Getting the campsite set up to Poppy's satisfaction had taken a while. The two tents were on one site, side by side, both facing away from the body of the camp. The food and cooking equipment was stowed in the car when they weren't using it and each tent had enough room for clothes and personal gear. They had decided not to spend Christmas day at the camp, but to have breakfast as soon as they were both awake, take day packs, drive to the beginning of the Abel Tasman track, and walk as far along it as they felt like and back. 'Bacon and eggs and fried bread is compulsory on the first morning,' Poppy announced. 'Couldn't do better in a British B & B,' was Jane's rejoinder.

They went together to find space in the camp fridge for their perishables and the freezer for their polar packs, then walked on the beach until it was dark, paddling on the edge of the sea. 'Cold,' was the shared verdict. It was Jane's turn to impress as they turned back towards the camp in the dark and she produced a small powerful torch from her pocket.

Both women hesitated slightly awkwardly at the edge of their camp site. Jane spoke first. 'Good night, sleep tight, don't let the bed bugs bite,' she said, and dived into her tent. Poppy could see her shadow moving about from the torch-light. Maybe this holiday could work after all, she thought, and was hardly in her sleeping bag before she fell asleep.

13

1999

On Christmas day Poppy woke to the hiss of the gas bottle. When she emerged Jane passed her a cup of hot coffee saying, 'I will not attempt to cook breakfast on this device yet but I can boil water!' They had agreed to leave the car key under the ground sheet at a corner of Poppy's tent and Jane had set out the cooker, table and rug. Before seven, only a few excited children were up and about, showing off a whole range of presents, most of which had wheels, so the two women made leisurely use of the ablution block showers.

After juggling, with a flourish, bacon, tomatoes, eggs and bread in one frying pan, and a pot, in front of an admiring audience of one, Poppy watched a perfectly fried egg, soft in the middle, slide off a flat spoon and splatter on the grass. 'Damn!'

Jane laughed. 'It's the look on your face,' she spluttered. With as much aplomb as she could manage, Poppy one-handedly broke another egg into the pan and carefully stacked the hot plates and the cooked food on top of the pot, with the pot lid on top of them. 'To keep them hot,' she explained unnecessarily, in a fair attempt at a dignified voice.

Jane insisted on taking the dishes over to the camp kitchen to wash up on her own. 'She who cooks does not wash up,' she announced firmly. Packing the cooker back in the car boot, Poppy caught a glimpse of a grinning Mrs Mudgely on the back seat. 'Well, I'm glad to see you can make it to the South Island,' she remarked to the vanishing image.

'We come to the South Island every Christmas.' She jumped and banged her head on the boot lid. 'Ouch!'

The small boy was holding a skateboard and the even smaller girl clung to his arm, wobbling on roller-blades.

'We always come, every year. Dad says when you live in Fielding you deserve two weeks a year at the sea. It takes ages to get here and she,' indicating his sister with a thumb, 'gets sick on the boat.'

'I did not, not for two years,' and she hit him on the arm. Then they were off, the boy carrying his skateboard under his arm with careful indifference and the girl stumbling across the bumpy ground.

'Christmas day at the beach, I can't believe it!' Jane went to put the plastic bowl of clean dishes into the boot. Poppy took it from her. 'If you put them in like that they'll rattle. Here, I'll show you.' And she used a tea-towel to wrap the cutlery and stacked everything neatly and firmly into its designated carton.

Seals swam and basked at two different points on their walk in the Abel Tasman National Park. While Poppy was disconcerted by the numbers of other people walking the track, Jane pronounced the 'crowds' to be, 'no worse than Scotland in August'. Their plan had been to leave the car at the park entrance, walk for a couple of hours and then retrace their steps. In the end they walked for six hours and, with breaks and two swims, were gone nearly nine hours. Arriving back at the camp too tired to cook, they finished the chicken with bread and tomatoes followed by an icecream from the store just as it closed at ten o'clock. They decided to spend Boxing Day around the camp and at the beach.

Feeling her stiff calf and thigh muscles in the morning, Poppy was glad of a light day to come and lay in her sleeping bag reading *The*

Poisonwood Bible until a trip to the toilet in the ablutions block became imperative. Coffee was ready again, a fruit salad assembled and fresh bread got from the store. Jane was sitting on a towel with her back to a small tree, writing in a notebook.

'Good morning. Shower first or breakfast?'

'Hi. Shower, I think, before the queues. This looks good.' Poppy indicated the food on May-Yun's table. 'I'll be right back.' They idled through the day, swimming, lying in the sun and the shade, reading, strolling on the beach.

As the afternoon went on Poppy noticed both parents and children around the camping ground becoming more fraught; children were crying, parents snapping. The family in the site next to theirs seemed comparatively unstressed, and Poppy kept an eye on them from behind her book. Both father and mother were active, engaging one or more of the three children with campsite tasks, intervening with distractions when squabbles among them were imminent. The children were active and far from quiet but their voices had none of the high-pitched, almost desperate quality of many others' and there were clearly preparations under way for an expedition of some kind. She was thinking about this, and about what proportion of how many families were actually having a good time when Jane, who had been studying at the map of Golden Bay, said, 'Let's go to Pupu Springs then explore the food options in Takaka'.

'Yes, great idea.' Poppy jumped up and threw her towel and book into her tent. Observing families at play was no real alternative.

The boardwalk and paths around the springs were easy walking and the setting postcard beautiful. Jane wanted to know the name of every fern and tree, and read every sign and every noticeboard; once again Poppy was aware of her own ignorance. She loved the feeling of places, the experience of being there and was not especially concerned with the names of things, while Jane concentrated on getting the facts before she relaxed into a place. How many million litres of water an hour bubbled, crystal clear, into the largest spring?

What was the water's path from the Takaka River and what caused variations in flow? How old were the rocks? 'Lots' was good enough answer for Poppy, unless she was in teacher mode. 'I'll bet Jane could get full marks in a test of what's in the signs,' she thought, examining a creature on a palm frond, speculating whether it was a moth or a butterfly and unconcerned which. She remembered childhood summer holidays with George and Katrina and Stefan, and felt nostalgic for the simple happinesses of her childhood.

Gazing into the water, disbelieving of its depth, enjoying the optical illusion of a bottom that was metres away but looked as though you could slice the water with your hand and touch it, Poppy saw, briefly, a smiling Mrs Mudgely.

'In 1993,' she said, glancing at Jane who was leaning on the rail beside her, 'a few months after I moved into my house, my friend Sara moved to live in Christchurch and I agreed to look after her cat Pussy, who was a dreadful traveller – she was impossible to put into a box and made horrendous noises if she was taken anywhere by car. Until Sara was settled in Christchurch was the idea. She had to drive the cat across town, loose in the car, to my place and when they arrived Sara was white and the cat walked in, jumped onto that chair she likes, kneaded it a few times, curled up with her nose under her tail and went to sleep.

'After a couple of days she deigned to acknowledge me and within a week she was waiting on the front steps for me when I came home from work.

'Sara discovered that her new partner, the woman she had moved to Christchurch to be with, was allergic to cats, which meant that Pussy would have had to live outside, so it was easy to suggest a full adoption – though I'm not sure who was adopting whom.

'I never liked "Pussy" as a name for her, she was a cat of too much character for such a nothing kind of name and right from the start she had reminded me of someone from a book I loved as a child. The book was called *The Peters Family*, I can never remember who wrote it, about this large family that lived in a big house in Kent, England, with stairs and cellars and attics, which I thought was so exotic, and there was a housekeeper who always helped the children when they got into scrapes – Stefan and I never had "scrapes" we just got into trouble – and comforted them when they were unhappy. So I started calling Pussy Mrs Mudgely after this character.

'Not long after that Katrina brought around a couple of boxes of things of mine she had kept. Now that I was settled, she said, I could decide for myself what I wanted to keep. And *The Peters Family* was in one of the boxes. I was hugely disappointed when I re-read it, the children were silly and prissy and their "scrapes" were things like getting their boots dirty and the housekeeper was patronising and pious. I wished I had never re-read it. The funny part, though, was that the housekeeper was actually Mrs Mudgeworth; I had remembered it wrong. Anyway, that's how Mrs Mudgely became Mrs Mudgely.'

When Poppy turned to look at Jane she saw an expression in her eyes that she could not identify. Each held the gaze for a moment, then looked away.

'Thank you for telling me that story. It is a lovely story, I am so glad to have heard it,' said Jane, very quietly.

'I don't usually tell it, I don't know what came over me,' said Poppy, and they were both silent again until they moved off in unspoken agreement as two young couples approached, pushing each other to the edges of the boardwalk, squealing and clutching when they nearly fell.

The café in Takaka was full, so they had to share a table with a young German couple who had been cycling around the North Island for a month and had just begun to do the same in the south. They chatted about the best places to go, and the sights they had seen and Poppy caught herself once again promoting the beauties of New Zealand with an earnestness that was close to embarrassing. She stopped abruptly. 'Oops, here I go again, ambassador for New Zealand scenery.'

'It is indeed very beautiful,' said the woman, 'we must go and sleep now, we will cycle back over that hill tomorrow. Goodnight, and thank you for your company.' The man nodded and smiled without saying anything.

Poppy and Jane finished their meal of chickpea loaf, baked potato and salad. 'Superb salad,' commented Jane, 'but I shan't ask for the loaf recipe.' They split the bill and headed back to their tents in fading light, discussing whether to do a day trip to Farewell Spit the next day, or head south. When they got back to the campground they found out that both Farewell Spit trips for the next day were full, but a third would go if they got ten names and so far there were four, not including them. 'I take it that's a "no",' said the man in the store as they shook their heads in unison. 'Okeydoke then,' and he put the exercise book back under the counter.

'It wasn't that funny.' Poppy was still laughing as she said it.

'I didn't want to hang about in the morning waiting,' said Jane when she had her breath back. 'I'm glad you didn't either. Of course it would have been fine if you had wanted ...'

Poppy's look silenced her.

The boy with the skateboard, still under his arm, and trailing a towel said 'Hi' to Poppy as he passed them on the path.

'Who's your friend?'

'A kid who ... oh, never mind. Look at that sunset!'

Jane went to watch the rest of the sunset from the beach, while Poppy decided she would write a few postcards. The car steering wheel was at the wrong angle for writing, but she managed to finish four cards before the light got too dim.

Driving down and about the West Coast over the next five days, they settled into a routine of travelling where they shared the driving and the non-driver chose the music tapes. Poppy had included a collection of classical and women's music; she tended to play the classical, having sung her way down the North Island to the women, while Jane was less familiar with the women's music genre, and 'extended my repertoire,' as she put it. Ferron and Sweet Honey in the Rock became her favourites. 'Thank goodness neither of us is crazy about heavy metal or country and western or anything else the other thinks is dreadful,' she commented as they left Greymouth. Poppy, driving at the time, nodded agreement and got to thinking about how compatible they were turning out to be, how easy it was to be in the car, them and the music, and go for long periods without talking.

Jane initiated most of the side trips; she continually gathered brochures and read them all and found places to see and walk – often in the rain – that Poppy had never heard of. The rain came in heavy showers but so far they had not had to pitch their tents in it, though one morning they had packed up tents wet from night rain. Jane gave up helping to pack the boot, Poppy was so particular about it. It wasn't that Jane did it 'wrong', it was that Poppy insisted on doing it a certain way. Jane thought about this often, how she had felt 'in the wrong' at least once practically every day in her life and not at all on this trip, unless she thought of Héloise.

One night, in her sleeping bag, she had cried quietly for a long time, at memories of her mother's comments that were never quite complaints; 'don't bother if …', and 'when you have a moment …', and 'don't go to any extra trouble for me …', and 'I'll manage, don't worry about me'. 'Odd,' she thought, groping about for tissues, 'the words could have been meant kindly, to be considerate …' But the tone was never kind or considerate. She shivered remembering her mother's voice in those last two years, always breathless, always with an edge that made Jane feel like a child, never smiling. Until the time her brother had come, for two days, and her mother had smiled and – fawned was the only word for it – and stroked his arm. Then he was gone again and the affection was switched off and the beseeching looks and clinging grasp and that tone of voice returned and Jane had felt the corroding resentment that deepened her guilt. Now she was having the same feelings, but it was Héloise beseeching and clinging; her own resentment and guilt were the same, familiar, deadening, helpless pall.

'Goodnight.' Poppy's voice was quiet, in case Jane was already asleep. Jane didn't answer in case her tears were in her voice. It took her a very long time to go to sleep.

On New Year's Eve they were sitting side by side on a bank of Lake Wanaka, with a bottle of cold white wine and the moon making brief appearances through the clouds. They knew when it was midnight from the noise at the camp behind them and held their glasses up to each other and clinked them, saying, 'Happy New Year,' in unison. They had agreed earlier that the millennium nature of the new year was something neither of them cared about, except for Jane's concerns about communication with home. They were silent again after their exchange of good wishes until Jane said, in a voice so low that Poppy was only just sure she had heard her, 'I think I am in love with you.'

Poppy's 'Oh,' was also barely audible. 'Um ... ah ...,' she couldn't find words for her chaotic smorgasbord of emotions, part surprise, part panic, part something warm, something she didn't want to know about right now, not with Héloise on the other side of the world part of the mix. At the thought of the implications of her warm feelings she felt a familiar gnaw in her stomach. At last she could manage, 'I don't know what to say ... I really like you ... there's all these other things ...'

'I know,' said Jane, 'especially living on opposite sides of the world, and most especially me having a partner.'

The moon was creeping out from behind a solid cloud, some wisps curling around its edges, a few stars visible across the sky, the whole setting impossibly romantic. Misery engulfed Poppy. It was as if one of the deep grey clouds had reached down and was clutching her stomach with an unbearably strong fist.

'I can't,' she said, 'I just can't, you know, get involved, even think about whether I want to … I can't get past her, you know, Héloise.' With a short laugh, she continued, 'Eve tells me I have what she calls a "fifties heterosexual morality" about relationships and I can see the irony in that for a lesbian, but it's not something rational, it's completely emotional and I can't even take the moral high ground with it, I just feel so absolutely miserable if I even contemplate being, you know, lovers, or anything, with someone in an existing relationship, or someone I am with being with someone else … I know it's probably some kind of arrested development, and I just can't help it. And in a way I don't want to. I never wanted to deal with it in therapy – that was Alexa's idea – it's just a part of me, and mostly I can live with it okay.' Poppy's voice faded away on the last words. Her arms were wrapped tightly around her bent legs.

'I'm not going to apologise for saying what I did.' This time Jane hesitated, with a small laugh. 'I had to say that to stop myself saying "I'm sorry". And I'm not.' Her voice got a little higher and a little tighter. 'So I guess I have to go back at the end of the month and sort out things there. In the meantime do you think we could go on having this holiday the way we were before … before I said anything?'

Without looking at her, Poppy nodded. Jane jumped up, and put her hand on Poppy's shoulder for a moment, and possibly, Poppy thought, kissed her on the top of her head. 'I'm off to bed,' she said, in that high, tight voice and walked off.

Still hugging her knees, Poppy sat following the movement of clouds in front of the moon with her eyes, holding herself motionless, waiting to see whether a recognisable emotion would emerge from the swirling soup that engulfed her. After a few minutes she gave up and went back to her tent. There was no torchlight in Jane's. Rather than join the melée in the ablutions block, Poppy cleaned her teeth with some water from her drinking bottle and climbed into her sleeping bag, expecting to lie awake for hours. Instead, she went to sleep almost instantly, and when she emerged in the morning Jane was up with coffee brewing, a bit heavy-eyed, otherwise seeming ordinary, and they did carry on just as they had before.

14

2000

Wanaka had held them for four days. Three of these had included long walks in the breathtakingly beautiful country. For hours they would walk, talking only occasionally, about where to stop for lunch, when to turn back or take a side path. From time to time the silences seemed strained to Poppy and then she would point out a particular view or plant or bird. Striding along the shore of Lake Tekapo one day, in single file determined by the track, she had touched Jane on the arm from behind, causing her to start and turn quickly, failing to hide her tears.

'Are you okay? You were setting a fierce pace there.'

'Yes. No. Well, yes, really.' Jane wiped her eyes with the back of a sleeve. 'Thinking about my life, what I must – want – to do. And affected by all this.' She waved at the lake and the mountains. 'I've never seen such colour in a lake, that turquoise blue against the tawny tussock, and the mountains in the back, and that blue, blue sky. I keep thinking it can't be real, it must be a scene in a film, carefully filtered for effect. And I'm not even wearing sunglasses! Sorry if I seem like I am bolting, would you like to go in front?'

Poppy shook her head. 'Why didn't I give her a hug?' she asked herself as they walked on, 'that was what I wanted to do, that's what

I would have done with any of my friends.' 'Because you are scared to,' she answered herself, and directed her attention to the dinghy out on the lake where a man was pulling in a fair-sized fish.

On every walk the backdrop was mountains, mountains with valleys of snow still, shining bright white in the day's sun, stained pink, yellow, orange, even red once, on those mornings and evenings with clouds around the horizon.

The routine became that Jane would set up the cooker in the morning and make coffee, get cereal and fruit ready and assemble a packed lunch. Poppy would make an evening meal, inventive with packets and tins, rice and pasta, always with salad. They shopped for fruit and salad items most days, stopping at roadside stalls and small towns.

When they had crossed to the eastern side of the island they lingered at the motor camp at Pounawea, with Jane, enraptured by the bird life, spending hours with her binoculars studying the estuary and practically bursting with delight when she saw spoonbills and godwits. The camp was small and full, mostly of 'people from the city who come every year', according to the proprietor, and Poppy realised the city he was talking about was Invercargill. The sites were generous, among mature rimu, as many as Poppy had ever seen in one place. The only space available to them was next to the track that led to the estuary, which meant they were woken early by campers going down for shellfish, but neither saw this as too high a price for the location. They gathered pipis themselves one afternoon and Poppy made a pasta sauce that she described as 'pretty close to a marinara' which Jane pronounced delicious, once she had overcome her inhibition at eating shellfish she had gathered herself.

Her excitement at the bird life was contagious and Poppy began looking out for birds in a different way and even beginning to identify them. It was the scenery, however, and the empty spaces that moved her most; driving for an hour without passing another car, walking on a track all day and seeing only two or three other parties, and them mostly just as inclined as she was to give a friendly smile and carry on without stopping to chat.

The weather was miserable when they got to Dunedin, cold and drizzly, with low cloud. There were a couple of women Poppy knew in the city and they badly needed to do some washing, so she rang one, who was leaving for a holiday in the North Island that day and reported the other was already in Australia for three weeks, so they found a Laundromat just off the road that ran through the centre of the city.

It wasn't until nearly the end of their second trip to Taiaroa Heads that they saw albatrosses flying. On their first visit they went to the albatross centre and on the (expensive, Poppy thought) guided tour where they saw two birds resting on the cliffside but none in the air. This time they were walking on the grassy hillside, discussing whether to give up and leave, as the cloud had been lifted for an hour or more, when Poppy spotted some movement over the sea and they watched as a Royal Albatross soared in and circled above their heads twice, followed soon after by another two. Jane stood motionless, her head bent back and moving slowly as she followed their path. When they were finally out of sight she straightened, tears running down her face. 'I have waited to see them flying in the wild for as long as I can remember,' she said. 'I have felt so much, so much, I don't know – joy – in this country, it's almost like I am coming to life again after a long sleep.' Poppy passed her a handful of tissues, smiling, and after a moment's hesitation put her arm around the other woman's shoulder and then they were hugging and laughing together, unaware of the people around them. Jane stepped back first.

They spent two nights at Sara's in Christchurch, one day walking in the Port Hills, new to them both, and relishing the contrast between the brown, baked hills, the blue of the harbour and the rugged, moody coastline they had just left to the south. Jane took advantage of the phone to make several off-peak calls to England. Poppy spent the evenings out with Sara and her friends, going to a movie and having dinner at the arts centre. They did the 'required walk' in the botanic gardens that Sara insisted on and Jane spent two fruitful hours at the arts centre market buying presents to take home. She was very taken with the museum, but as it was a Saturday there were no staff there for her to talk with, which, once she had enquired, was a relief; she already had more information than she could deal with to take home. The three of them lunched together in the museum café.

Jane was disappointed when they discovered that the whale watch expeditions from Kaikoura were fully booked for the next day, when they would be travelling along the coast to Picton. Poppy apologised for not taking more account of the holiday season and suggesting they book ahead.

'Never mind. I'm sure I'll be back ...' Jane stopped. Sara was looking from one to the other. Jane noticed and continued in a rush. 'This is not a country where you can do everything in one visit. What time to we need to leave for the ferry?'

'The day before, we sail at six a.m.' Poppy knew her face had reddened and looked steadily at the table as she continued, 'We could stay overnight at the same place as we did on the way down; let's not have to pack up our tents at four in the morning.'

'Tents?' Sara was smiling. 'One each, huh? That's the Poppy I know and love.'

'You haven't even asked about your ex-cat,' said Poppy suddenly, desperate for a change of subject.

'Oops, I haven't given her a thought for ages. How is she?' Jane watched Sara watching Poppy as the latter talked about Mrs Mudgely, clearly telling Sara more than she wanted to hear.

The next day was cloudy with occasional light showers as they drove north along the coast. They didn't talk much. Jane spotted a seal on the rocks near Kaikoura and they stopped and watched that for a while.

When the ferry entered Cook Strait there was a big enough swell to rock the boat; Poppy felt queasy and went and sat in the bottom lounge where the movement was slightest. Jane stayed outside as long as she could, watching the sun rise and the South Island recede. She had been pleased at the opportunity to undertake this expedition to New Zealand, both to revitalise her in her work and, she knew from the beginning, to have time away from Héloise to think about her own reactions to the idea of a child and their future together.

She would go back a different person. 'What an odd idea,' she told herself at the thought, 'of course I'm not a different person. I've just changed a lot inside.' She watched the black-backed gulls swooping over the ship, enjoying the sensation of soaring with them. Tears came to her eyes when she realised this was a new response to watching sea birds; previously she had envied them their flight, their freedom. She opened her arms wide and swung them in unison with the wings of the nearest gull, starting when a voice behind her said, 'You're not thinking of jumping, are you miss?' 'No, no, of course not, I was just … never mind.' and she moved off, flustered and embarrassed.

The ship rolled in the swell, and she nearly lost her footing. Moving inside she found a seat by a window and started composing an email to Héloise in her head. Should she tell her about her feelings for Poppy now, or wait until she got home and could tell her in person? Or on the phone? No, not on the phone. She stared at her reflection in the window and the sea beyond, remembering the early days with Héloise when they had been happy, had both wanted to live the same life, trying to find the time when that had changed, to identify exactly when she herself had begun to feel constrained and resentful of what had become to her an increasingly unwelcome domestic and, well, boring, life. And how long had this been going on without her being aware of it? This was her greatest concern, her own not knowing what she wanted, falling so easily into pleasing the people around her, oblivious to her creeping discontent. She stared out the window until she saw the hills around the entrance to Wellington Harbour, then went to find Poppy, who she discovered sitting in the middle of the downstairs lounge, slightly pale, turning the pages of a magazine.

'Okay?' she asked, sitting beside her.

'Just.' Poppy managed a weak smile. 'This rock and roll should stop as soon as we are in the harbour and I'll be glad of that. I've been doing my best not to imagine us all at the bottom of the sea with our grieving relatives on the shore, but I couldn't tell you a single thing in this,' and she tossed the magazine onto an empty seat.

They did not linger in Wellington.

'Been there, done that,' Jane said. She was driving off the ferry.

'You're starting to talk like a New Zealander, must be time you went home. A few weeks ago you would have said, "I do not need to spend any more time in Wellington, thank you, if that is all right with you",' adding, 'Sorry, bad taste comment,' when she became aware of Jane's shoulders stiffening. 'Just teasing and thoughtlessly in the circumstances, I'm sorry.' And Poppy fell silent, thinking how easily she slipped into teasing Jane and how she had always so hated being teased herself that she never did it to anyone else and wondering why she did it to Jane. She waited a moment to see if Mrs Mudgely would help her. She didn't. Apart from the two times in Golden Bay, she had not appeared all trip. Poppy sighed and Jane looked around at her.

'Missing Mrs Mudgely,' she explained, 'silly, really.'

'I missed my – our – dog, Benjy, like mad at first. Goodness, I've hardly thought of him in the last few weeks! Oh golly, which lane do I take along here, are we going to the Hutt Valley or Po – the other way.'

'Hutt, Masterton, Wairarapa, that way, Highway 2. I think. Where do you want to stop?'

'Napier. Or Hastings, or Havelock North.'

'Whoa, that's something like five hours' drive, and we wouldn't get there until nearly dark, and it's a really popular holiday area, I don't know how easy it will be to find a camping ground that's not full …'

'Leave it to me,' Jane was firm. 'If that petrol station up ahead has a public phone, I'll make some calls.' They were on the road to the Hutt Valley and the petrol station was on its own, no surrounding shops or other services, so Poppy doubted the phone. 'Putting up the tents after dark is a pain,' she said, 'how about we go as far as Woodville, or even Dannevirke, we should be about to do that before dark …' Poppy was leafing through the camping guide, aware that in the more heavily-populated North Island, driving up and finding a place with an empty campsite might not be so easy.

'Let me make a phone call first.' Jane was pulling in to the petrol station. She set the pump on 'fill', picked up her purse and held out her hand for the camping guide. She was gone several minutes and came back grinning, clearly pleased with herself. 'I hope you don't mind,' she said, getting back behind the wheel, 'I've organised us a cabin at a motor camp on the way to Cape Kidnappers for two nights.' She was pulling out into the heavy late-afternoon traffic. 'It was the third place I rang and I had nearly given up, and I've cleaned out all my coins, but they had a late cancellation about an hour ago. We have to be there by ten o'clock tonight.'

'But I thought …'

'I know, camping all the way. But this way we won't have to set up camp in the dark and we'll have all day tomorrow to go to the gannet colony. And never mind the cost, this is on me, I've already put it on my credit card so they would be sure and keep the cabin for us. Seriously, though, do you mind?'

'No, I don't mind at all, in fact I'm a bit relieved. I'm tired from feeling sick on the ferry, I think. Maybe I should take my turn at driving now, while I can still keep my eyes open. And I'll pay my share of the cabin, really, I want to do that.'

'If you insist, but no driving. This expedition – or section of the expedition – comes complete with driver.' Her voice dropping a little, Jane went on, 'I think I'm practising being assertive, making things I want happen. Which is rather sad when you think about it, but at least I'm doing it before I am forty, if only by a few months. So madam,' and she swung over to the fast lane, 'sit back and enjoy the ride.'

They arrived at the camping ground at ten to ten. Neither woman had realised how private each had been in her separate tent, and how little privacy there would be in a tiny one-room cabin. They were awkwardly quiet unpacking the car and getting ready to sleep and climbed gratefully into bed, both lying awake for some time and each wanting the other to think she was asleep. In the morning Poppy woke early and crept out of her sleeping bag, gathering clothes and towel as she went. When she got outside and saw how close the sea was and felt the warmth of the morning sun, she snuck back in for her swimming togs. She swam out into the bay, enjoying the warmer, northern water, floating on her back, idly speculating on the identity of various birds flying overhead on their morning business, watching some, terns maybe, diving for fish further out. Remembering that they had to set out for the gannet colony by nine o'clock to catch the low tide, she turned over and began the swim to shore. This was how she enjoyed the sea, calm, on a warm day, immersed and in her depth.

It was a full five hour excursion to the gannets, easy walking on the beach, with many pauses while Jane used her binoculars, frequently passing them to Poppy, who was fairly certain which was a gannet and which a seagull. The black-backed gulls were easy, they were so big and their black wings so bold. The cliffs were spectacular, shapes carved out of the soft sand and shingle by sea and wind and fragmented and tilted by the many earthquakes in their history. Once again, it seemed to Poppy, Jane entered a kind of rapture watching the birds, motionless for long minutes, then swaying slightly as if in imitation of their flight. Over their lunchtime sandwiches, Poppy asked why Jane never took photographs, of either the birds or the scenery; the few shots from this trip were on Poppy's camera, 'I never have,' the other woman replied, 'birds are so difficult without expensive equipment and I could never afford that. And the grandeur, the majesty, all that gets lost. I hold the pictures in my mind I suppose and remember what I saw and the whole feeling, the experience, of being there.'

173

Poppy decided that she wanted a rest and a swim more than to do the full walk to the gannet colony, so Jane went on alone. They had agreed to both be back at the car by six, and Jane only just made it. She flopped into the passenger seat, 'That was one of the wonderful experiences of my life.' Her face was glowing. 'I've seen the big colony at St Kilda once, and spent lots of time watching gannets at Bempton Cliffs – that's on the coast south of Scarborough – but this was magic. Some of the fledglings are fishing for themselves already. The water was boiling in places, there were so many birds diving. And the headland. And the sky, oh, I just can't tell you how wonderful it all was. And the walk. I spent so long there I had to hurry back, you weren't worried were you?'

Poppy shook her head. 'Nope. I've swum and lazed and read a bit. It's great to see you enjoy yourself so much. How about I drive us in to Napier and we find a beer.' They admired the art deco buildings and bought some cold cans then found a Chinese take-away and sat on the foreshore. As they finished, and began to gather up the cartons and wrappings Jane asked Poppy, tentatively, whether she would mind if they did not spend the next week wending their way around the east cape, but went more directly back to Auckland. 'I'm feeling guilty about how little I have communicated with Héloise since Christmas and it's hard to not tell her, um, things that are going on for me, and hard to tell her when it's not easy to phone. I thought I could leave things until I get home, but I don't think I can. And I am thinking I will see if I can go back a week earlier. I don't want to though, yet I do want to at the same time.'

'Are you saying you want to cut this trip short?'

Jane looked miserable. 'No, I want it to go on forever. But that is just not possible. And it is getting, well, harder, being together so much and feeling ... the way I do ... and not ... and there is everything at home. I am so torn, yet I know what I have to – want to – do, and I suppose I know I should get on and do it and being on holiday isn't doing it. Am I making any sense at all.'

'Yes, perfectly good sense. And I haven't been helping. I really, honestly don't know about my feelings right now. I really really like you.' Poppy's laugh was tinged with ruefulness, 'and I seem to be incapable of doing more than that while things are as they are. I'm not just being difficult, I just don't seem to be able to be any different, and that's not fair. So yes, let's go to Auckland – tomorrow? the next day?'

'The next day. One final night in those bloody, monastic tents! You choose where. If you don't mind, that is.'

'What if I do mi … – oops, I've got to curb my new tendency to tease, I don't understand it at all – of course I don't mind choosing where. Let's see. Not Taupo, that will be totally crowded and awful, I know, Rotorua – can you stand the smell of rotten eggs for one night?' Jane nodded. 'Right, then. Damn! the camping guide is back at the cabin.'

'No, it isn't.' Jane produced it from her shoulder bag.

'Armed with this and my trusty phone card, I will venture forth and return with news,' and Poppy was off across the road looking around for a phone booth. She returned a few minutes later having secured a site at a place on the way into Rotorua for the following night. 'Hey, I passed the movie theatre and Ants is showing in fifteen minutes, wanna go?'

'Ants?'

'Ants. A cartoon movie about a radical ant. Annie raved about it.'

'Okay then.'

They laughed at the same places in the movie, and drove back to the cabin chatting about it and other movies they had seen, more relaxed with each other now that they had changed their plans. It remained so over the next two days' driving and their night near Rotorua. They celebrated their last night camping with steak cooked on the gas cooker, salad and a bottle of Marlborough wine, making easy conversation about their childhood experiences, work and friends, without reference to the present or the future.

Stopping only at Moggy Manor in Drury to collect Mrs Mudgely, who rode home on Poppy's lap while Jane drove in on the motorway, they pulled up outside the Mt Eden house just after one o'clock. Once unpacked, with the camping gear stowed in the laundry until the drizzle stopped, Poppy embarked on a series of phone calls letting people know she was back. At that time of day she was giving the information to answerphones, which saved her from multiple explanations. Martia, however, was home and her tired voice and dispirited replies were alarming. Katrina was in also, and her news was that she had sent Mr 'Smart by nature' packing and when could they have lunch and she would tell Poppy all about it.

'Are you okay, Katrina?'

'Oh yes, my dear, I'm quite okay, thank you. It's that Mr Smarty-pants who's not okay. He should have known better than to ask my friends for money for his shonky investments.' They arranged to have brunch together in Ponsonby Road the next day. 'Saturday brunch in Ponsonby Road,' thought Poppy, 'welcome back to the big city.' She heard the cat flap and called out to Mrs Mudgely who came in and jumped on the bed beside her. 'I missed you, Mrs M.' Poppy scratched her between the ears and was rewarded by the first purr since she had collected her. 'That was more than a holiday, that was, with you out of range or sulking, and me floundering about in my emotions. I did all right, though – mostly anyway – and walked some long and lovely walks and saw some new and wonderful sights in that South Island.' She continued her murmuring and stroking the cat until she heard the door, and went to help with the bags of groceries.

'I got a weekends' worth,' Jane had four supermarket bags in each hand.

'It must be a long weekend, then – here, give me some.' There was a bit of a flurry when Jane couldn't find the car keys, which turned up in her pocket. Once the groceries were put away, Jane asked whether she could use the computer for a while, 'to check my email and then write some. What about you, you want to check yours?' Poppy shook her head. 'Nah, there won't be anything urgent, anyone who matters thinks I'm still away.' She grinned. 'You go ahead, I'll rustle up a quick meal, then I want to go and see Martia, she sounds awful and I think she's either sick or miserable or both.

The phone rang twice while they were eating the pasta, pesto and salad Poppy had prepared, as people returned her calls and wanted a full story, so there was no opportunity to talk as they ate. Alexa and Bessie were coming around the following afternoon and May-Yun invited them both to dinner. 'That's tomorrow, then, Katrina for brunch, Alex and Bess in the afternoon and May-Yun's for dinner.' Jane looked alarmed. 'I'm not sure I ...'

'There's no obligation for dinner, we just turn up if we feel like it, one or both. And if you don't want to be grilled by A and B you could always go for a walk. Look, you've got all your own stuff to deal with, you don't have to involve yourself with my friends and family any more than you want. No-one is going to have a hissy fit if you're otherwise occupied.'

Jane had turned her face away. She sniffed. 'Sorry to be pathetic. I'm still not used to ... you are very kind, and, well undemanding, and that means I have to know what I want! I want to enjoy this trip and being with you,' her smile was apologetic, 'and your friends and family. And that is not possible, I suppose, without dealing with everything else. I could use someone to talk to, but I suspect you would not be the best choice.' Poppy was nodding her agreement. 'I am missing my good friend at home as someone to talk to.' Jane was crying and smiling at the same time. 'I must look terrrible.'

'Just hang on a minute.' Poppy picked up the phone, tapped in some numbers, listened, tapped some more. When she put down the phone she said. 'I thought so. There's a $10 cap on calls to Britain off-peak all weekend starting,' she looked at her watch, 'ten minutes ago. Call your friend. Call whoever you need to.' She put on an artificial voice, 'Calls can be for up to six hours and cost no more than ten dollars.' She held up a hand to stop Jane's response. 'I'm off to Martia's. Use the phone and the computer as much as you want.'

'That's what you call bolting,' Poppy said to Mrs Mudgely, who was on her bed, as she collected a jacket. Mrs Mudgely was inscrutable. 'You're leaving me to this one on my own aren't you, madam cat? I love you anyway,' and with one long stroke from the cat's ears to the tip of her tail, she was gone.

The smell of onions cooking raised Poppy's hopes as she knocked on the open front door and headed for the kitchen of Martia's house. They fell abruptly when she saw her friend's pale face and drooping shoulders. She cheered visibly when she saw Poppy, and put down the knife she was using to chop vegetables to hug her. 'My god, you've lost weight!' Poppy stood back from the hug and looked at her friend. 'You look awful.'

'And hello to you, too.' Martia's sigh came from her whole body. 'It's great to see you, and you look disgustingly cheerful and healthy like someone who has been on holiday. Tell me about it while I finish this; Barb's due home soon and I said I'd cook. Will you join us.'

'Thanks, but I just ate. How about I give you a hand while I catch you up with my goings on and then we can sit down and talk about you.' They prepared and cooked the stir-fry companionably while Poppy told travel stories, leaving out for the time being the events of New Year's Eve. When Barb came in she was talking before she entered the room.

'Looks like we have a visitor there's a car ... oh, hi Poppy. Hello doll,' she glanced at Martia and crossed to the stove. 'Great, it looks just about ready. I've got to eat and dash, I've got the boss's wife's ticket to a charity movie tonight, she's gone down with some lurgy. Apparently the movie's not up to much, but it's a great opportunity to mix and mingle with the rich and famous. Hey, I'll go check my wardrobe for something to wear, give me a yell when it's done.' The two friends said little until Barb had gone. Martia pushed the food around her plate without eating most of it.

When they were finally sitting on the sofa, Poppy with coffee, Martia with herbal tea, Poppy faced her friend and said 'Okay, now tell me all about everything.' Martia shrugged, her hands palm up in a gesture of hopelessness, then buried her face in them and openly cried. Her own eyes filling with tears Poppy put her arms around her friend and held her, patting her back and making soothing murmurs until the sobs subsided.

'Oh Poppy, I just can't cope any more, and I don't know what to do. I always know what to do for other people and I can't think what to do for myself and yet, there's nothing really, except I've got no energy and I feel really, really miserable and I've had to give up my job at the refuge so now I'm back on a benefit – at least my doctor has gotten me a sickness benefit rather than the dole – and she, the doctor, wants me to take anti-depressants and I'm so scared of doing that, look what happened to my mother, and everything is just closing in on me and I can't think …'

'So where's Barb in all this?'

'Oblivious. Wrapped up in her own life. No, that's not really fair, she more than pays her way and tries to cheer me up by asking me to go out to things with her, you know social events and clubs. Places I didn't enjoy when I felt well,' she ended bitterly. 'But I have to be fair, she does her best, and the deal between us never included this,' she gestured again, helplessly. 'Honestly it took me all afternoon to get dinner. Once I'd have done it in between work and a meeting talking on the phone.'

'What does the doctor say about the tiredness and everything?'

Martia gave another big sigh. 'That it could be a hormonal thing, menopause and all that, or ME or chronic fatigue syndrome or depression. She's had some tests done and apparently I don't have any signs of cancer or diabetes or anaemia or a couple of other things I forget.'

Poppy kept asking questions until she couldn't think of any more. At no time did Martia say anything that suggested she might have any idea about what to do about her situation, which alarmed Poppy, who had seen her friend being competent and in charge so often she

179

assumed she could manage anything. One recurring theme was lack of money, which led Poppy to thinking about her own good fortune in having fall-back options with both her parents and probably even her brother.

'Martia, if you were able to do anything at all, go anywhere, what would it be, where would you go? No, don't tell me the difficulties again, just tell me your wish list.'

'I would go to my ex-sister-in-law's, she's farming rare animal breeds, goats and sheep and pigs I think, north of Whangarei, with a woman actually. I saw her at Christmas, she came to pick up her kids and she offered me a caravan if I wanted a holiday. I would have gone, but my car needs at least one new tyre before I can get a warrant of fitness, so I can't drive it.'

'Right, Here's a plan.' Poppy held up a hand to stop Martia saying anything. 'I'll take your car off on Monday and get it warranted. You ring your sister-in-law and talk to Barb. You can leave on Tuesday – in fact, my plan just got better – I'll drive you up, Jane can bring my car, maybe, – yes, this is turning into a beautiful plan! What are you giggling at?'

'You sound just like Katrina.'

'Oh shit. Well, if I start calling you 'dear', just pinch me, here.' Poppy indicated the tender flesh on the inside of her upper arm.

'But Poppy, I can't let you …'

'Yes you can,' she replied firmly. 'Think of it as pay-back time.'

'For …?'

'Everything. Every time you have got anyone, including me – especially me – through something awful and all that work you have done in rape crisis and refuge instead of earning real money. Let me do this, please Martia.'

Both women were crying now. 'All right,' snuffled Martia.

By Monday lunchtime it was all arranged. Martia's car had two new front tyres, a warrant of fitness and a full petrol tank. The pre-paid cell phone was Katrina's idea, and she provided it, with a hundred dollars' worth of calls. 'There won't be a proper phone in a caravan,' Katrina had pronounced. 'These things chomp through the money at a fast clip so tell her to encourage people to ring her to chat, then they pay through the nose.'

May-Yun contributed a care parcel that included a fruit cake she had baked herself and Stefan added a strong torch. 'You never know when you'll need one in the country. She's a good person, that friend of yours, give her my best.' Her family's generosity, which she had largely taken for granted over the years, made Poppy feel both humbled and glad. Humbled because she fallen into the habit of noticing mainly their faults, and glad that she had had the good fortune to be born into a family that was more or less functional and well enough off financially, unlike Martia and a number of her other friends.

She had arranged with Jane, who said little of her communications home except that she had had a long talk to her friend and that had been a very good idea, that Jane would take her car north and have a couple of days on her own in the Bay of Islands, meeting Poppy at Tahere about mid-day on Thursday. Martia and Poppy would drive to the farm, near Whangarei, on the Wednesday and Poppy would stay overnight with her in the caravan.

The plan was for Martia to be away a month and then decide what she would do next. Barb did not seem to Poppy to take any interest in their plans, apart from telling Martia that a holiday would do her good.

Poppy was relieved that her friend was in slightly better spirits, though her energy continued to be low. The responsibility of intervening in someone else's life bothered Poppy, until May-Yun pointed out to her that not intervening could leave one just as responsible.

Before she left for the far north at lunchtime on Monday, Jane told Poppy that she had managed to change her flight, so she would be leaving a week earlier, on January 22nd. 'I wish you were coming to Northland with me.' Jane did not look at Poppy while she said this. 'But I suppose it is for the best. And you are very generous to let me

181

take your car. At least, I suppose, you know my driving and I promise I'll take care.' She drove off and Poppy went inside to see whether there was anything that was going to jump out and bite her in the one hundred and thirty-five emails she had downloaded the day of her return and not got around to reading, except for one from George, wanting to know, among other things, how she and Jane were getting along. 'Can't answer that, George, at this moment,' she said to herself as she ran up the steps.

She discovered that more than half the emails awaiting her attention were from a couple of queernet lists she thought she had unsubscribed from before she went away. She opened one at random and read, 'Greetings, Radical Queers!' then deleted it. Going through the list, deleting any from the same or a similar source, she wondered why she had such a strong reaction to being called 'queer'. 'Lesbian' was a label she accepted easily now, but 'queer' made her uneasy. 'I don't want to be queer,' she said to Mrs Mudgely, who was in her usual place on the bed, 'I want to be a lesbian, I am a lesbian, an ordinary goddam lesbian.' Mrs M was up and stretching. 'Don't go, I won't shout any more, I promise.' Poppy stroked the cat until she lay down again and rolled over, offering her stomach. 'You see,' said Poppy, stroking the soft underside fur, 'being a lesbian is being something, you know, something identifiable, something concrete, even simple. And it's different from being heterosexual, it's not "normal" if normal is heterosexual, it's another way of being in the world, and it is different and it is an alternative to having a man so I guess it is kind of radical, but it's also ordinary. Being queer, well, that can be just about anything. Which is fine if that's what you want. But I don't, and if that means I'm underdeveloped, well, so be it.' By now Mrs Mudgely was sound asleep and Poppy went back to her email and started writing to George.

For the first hour of the drive back to Auckland Jane described what she had seen and done in the previous three days. 'I never thought I could get tired of scenery,' she was concluding, 'but I was thinking yesterday, that one more stunning view would just about make my eyes and brain explode. This country has so many different kinds of beautiful and they are all so close together, a person can only just stand it.'

'I guess you have seen a lot in a short time. Familiar old Yorkshire will be something of a relief then.'

'I would not go that far. I am quite anxious about going home. Work is not going to be easy, either; people have very high expectations of what I will bring back in the way of ideas and innovations and I don't think they have any idea at all of the costs. My friend Emma, the one you suggested I ring, thought it would be best if I did not talk to you much about me and Héloise and I suppose she is right. Can I keep in touch with you though?'

'Yes, please. I want you to. Very much.' Not leaving any time for a response, Poppy went on, 'Tomorrow is your last full day. What do you want to do?'

Jane replied, after a pause, 'I would like to make a picnic lunch on Maungawhau – see I can finally say it – and I hope you will come and your brother's family and Eve and Katrina, and Peter and a few others from the museum, oh, and Alexa and Bess. There is this spot, on the other side of the crater, that is really sheltered from the wind and I have been there a lot. And I have a confession to make.'

Poppy raised her eyebrows in a question.

'I have already asked your family and Eve – I phoned them from Whangarei – and they are all coming. I do hope you will.'

'Of course.' Poppy laughed with relief. 'I would be delighted. I'll help, with the food and everything.'

'No need. I have it all arranged. Oh, your car would be useful in the morning.'

About half the people who went to the picnic were at the airport to see Jane off the following day. Poppy couldn't decide whether having such a crowd there made saying goodbye easier or harder. All of a sudden Jane was gone down the air-bridge and Katrina was organising them to coffee at Poppy's house.

Three days later Poppy looked at jane.blackie in the 'who' column of her email inbox and smiled, a full, wide smile. Mrs Mudgely, who was curled up on the second spare bed, apparently asleep, raised her head, opened her eyes, and smiled just as widely.